Carol Marinelli recently filled in a form where she was asked for her job title and was thrilled, after all these years, to be able to put down her answer as 'writer'. Then it asked what Carol did for relaxation. After chewing her pen for a moment Carol put down the truth—'writing'. The third question asked: 'What are your hobbies?' Well, not wanting to look obsessed or, worse still, boring, she crossed the fingers on her free hand and answered 'swimming and tennis'. But, given that the chlorine in the pool does terrible things to her highlights, and the closest she's got to a tennis racket in the last couple of years is watching the Australian Open, I'm sure you can guess the real answer!

Books by Carol Marinelli

Unwrapping Her Italian Doc
Playing the Playboy's Sweetheart
200 Harley Street: Surgeon in a Tux
Tempted by Dr Morales
The Accidental Romeo
Secrets of a Career Girl
Dr Dark and Far Too Delicious
NYC Angels: Redeeming the Playboy

**Visit the author profile page at
millsandboon.co.uk for more titles**

Praise for Carol Marinelli

'A compelling, sensual, sexy, emotionally packed, drama-filled read that will leave you begging for more!'
—*Contemporary Romance Reviews* on
NYC Angels: Redeeming the Playboy

CHAPTER ONE

Before

'You paged me to see a patient.'

'No, I didn't.' Candy, holding an armful of sheets, smiled when it would have been far easier to stand there and gape. He was stunning—tall, slender, wearing a suit and a tie. His dark brown hair was cut short and his voice was so deep and commanding that it stopped Candy in her tracks. She met his chocolate-brown eyes fully and it took a moment to respond normally. 'Who are you here to see?'

'A Mr Thomas Heath.'

Candy walked over to the board. Emergency at the London Royal Hospital was quiet this afternoon but as she was in Resuscitation Candy didn't know which patients were in the cubicles. After a quick scan of the board, she located Mr Heath. 'He's in cubicle seven. Trevor's the nurse looking after him. He must be the one who paged you.'

'Thanks for that. By the way I'm Steele.'

'Steele?'

He watched as her very blue eyes moved to his name

badge. 'Well, Dr Guy Steele, if you'd prefer to be formal,' he said.

'Steele will do.' She must look like a dental commercial, Candy thought, for she simply couldn't stop smiling at him. He must be thirty or mid-thirties, which was a lot more than her twenty-four years, and he was also way older than anyone she had ever fancied, yet he had this impact, this presence, that had Candy's heart galloping in her chest.

'And you are?' he asked.

'Candy. Candy Anastasi.' She watched a smile twitch on his lips as she said her name. 'I know, I know, I should be tall, leggy and blonde to carry off a name like that!' Instead, she was short and a bit round with long black ringlets and piercing blue eyes. 'There's a story there.'

'I can't wait to hear it, Nurse Candy.'

He had the deepest voice that she'd ever heard. Like a headmaster, he was stern and bossy, yet it was all somehow softened by a very beautiful mouth that she could barely drag her eyes from. 'You'll never hear the story of my name,' Candy said.

'Oh, we'll have to see about that.'

Had they been flirting? Candy wondered as sexy-as-hell Steele walked off.

'Who's that?' Kelly said as they started to strip one of the resuscitation beds.

'Steele!' Candy said in a deep low voice, making Kelly laugh. She continued speaking gruffly while they bent over and tucked the sheet in. 'Or Dr Guy Steele if we want to be formal and, young lady, I'm going to make your eardrums reverberate with my deep—'

'Nurse Candy?'

Candy froze when she realised that Steele was be-hind her.

'Could I borrow your stethoscope?' he asked.

She laughed at being caught impersonating him and turned around and took her stethoscope from her neck and held it out to him, yet pulled back as he went to take it. 'You can,' she said, the stethoscope hovering. 'Just so long as you stop calling me Nurse Candy.'

He just took the stethoscope, smiled and walked off.

They made up all the beds and checked the crash trolleys and then gave up pretending to be busy, given that Lydia, the manager, was in her office. Instead, they took a jug of iced tea to the nurses' station, where Steele was tapping away on the computer. It was a lovely early summer day but the air-conditioning was struggling and it was nice to sit on the bench and gossip, though Steele had a couple of questions for her.

'How do you get into the pathology lab to check results?' he asked, not looking around.

'You've got your password?' Candy checked.

'I have and I've got into…' He tapped again. 'Got it.'

'Have you told your parents about Hawaii yet?' Kelly asked Candy, resuming the conversation they'd been having in the kitchen as they'd made their drink.

'No.'

'You go in four weeks' time,' Kelly pointed out.

'They might not notice that I've gone,' Candy said hopefully, then let out a sigh. Her parents were Italian, strict and very prone to popping over to her flat unannounced. They also spoke every day on the phone. 'I know I'll have to tell them or I'll be listed on Interpol as a missing person.'

Candy had, on a whim, booked a holiday to Hawaii.

Well, it hadn't been purely on a whim—she had already been aware that she needed to get away when the infomercial had appeared on her screen with a very special offer for the first ten callers. She'd been tired, a bit jaded and upset over a stupid fling with Gerry, one of the head nurses here. Thankfully he was in Greece for a couple of months, which spared Candy her blushes, but when she'd reached for the phone and, lucky her, been amongst the first ten callers, she'd known she needed this break.

She couldn't wait for two weeks in which to lie on a beach and explore the stunning island at leisure while she attempted to sort out a few things that were on her mind.

'They're going to freak when I tell them,' Candy admitted. 'They know that I can't really afford it.'

'It's all paid for?' Kelly checked, and Candy nodded.

'All except for spending money, but I've just spoken to the hospital bank and I've got loads of shifts. Actually, I haven't got a single day off until I fly.'

'Where are your shifts?'

'In the geriatric unit.'

Kelly pulled a face. 'Yuk.'

Candy didn't mind. She had enjoyed working in the geriatric unit during her training and was really grateful for the extra work. Even if she was exhausted at the prospect of nearly four more weeks without so much as a day off.

As her parents would point out, when she finally got around to it and told them about her holiday, it was foolish to be working extra shifts because you were so tired that you needed a break—but Candy just wanted to get away for a while.

'When do you start working there?'

'The weekend. I'm working Friday night and then I've got a four-hour shift on Sunday morning, then back here Monday.'

'Okay.' Steele turned around. 'I want Mr Heath pulled over to Resus. He needs to be monitored while I start him on some medication. His bloodwork's dire.'

'Sure.' Candy jumped down from the bench and she and Trevor brought Mr Heath over.

Candy wrote his name on the whiteboard and turned to Steele. 'Sorry, what specialty is he under?'

'Geriatrics,' Steele said, then he gave her a thin smile. 'Yuk!'

Candy's cheeks went pink; she wanted to point out that she hadn't been the one who had said that.

'It's okay,' Steele relented when he saw her uncomfortable expression. 'You hit a nerve—I hear that sort of thing a lot.'

'So are you a new geriatric consultant?' Kelly asked, but Steele shook his head.

'No, I'm only here temporarily. I'm covering for six weeks while Kathy Jordan is on extended leave.'

'Just six weeks?' Kelly asked shamelessly.

'Yep,' Steele said, and walked off.

'Wow, talk about bringing the schmexy into geriatrics,' Kelly said. 'And you're going to be working there, you lucky thing. I bet you're not complaining now.'

She hadn't been complaining in the first place, Candy was tempted to point out.

They soon paid for the lull in patients because, not an hour later, the department had filled and she and Kelly were busy in Resus, Kelly with a very ill baby and Candy attempting to calm down Mr Heath. He was rather shaky from the medication and was getting increasingly distressed and trying to climb down from the resuscitation bed.

'The medicine makes your heart race, Mr Heath,' Candy tried to explain to the gentleman. 'It will settle down soon…' But he couldn't understand what she said and kept trying to climb off the bed so Candy tried speaking louder. 'The medicine—'

'You do it like this.' Steele saw that she was struggling and came over. 'Mr Heath!' he boomed.

The people in the Waiting Room surely heard him, Candy thought as he gave the same explanation to Mr Heath that she had been trying to give. The gentleman nodded weakly in relief and then lay back on the pillows. 'Good man,' Steele barked and smiled at Candy and, in a comparatively dulcet tone, added, 'I have the perfect voice for my job.'

'You do,' she agreed.

'So you're going to be doing a few shifts up on the geriatric unit?'

'Yep.'

'For a holiday that you can't really afford?'

'I know,' Candy groaned.

'Well, good for you,' Steele said, and Candy blinked in surprise. 'Okay, once Mr Heath's medication has finished I want him monitored for another hour down here. Then everything's sorted for him to be admitted. We're just waiting on a bed, which might be a couple of hours. I've spoken to the ward and they have said that they'll ring down when they're ready for him to come up.'

'Ha-ha,' Candy said, because there was no way that

the ward was likely to ring down. Instead, she would have to chase them and push for the bed to be readied.

Steele well understood her sarcastic comment. 'Well, I hope that they do ring down in a timely manner. I'm less than impressed with the waiting times for patients to get into a bed at the Royal.'

With that he stalked off, possibly to return to whatever fluffy white cloud he'd just drifted down from, Candy thought.

She'd never, ever been so instantly captivated by someone.

Candy left Kelly watching Mr Heath when she was told to go for her lunch break. She'd forgotten to bring lunch so she bought a bag of salt-and-vinegar crisps from the vending machine and put them between two slices of bread and butter. Sitting down in the staff-room, she smiled at Trevor, who was having his lunch too, and checked her phone. Yes, her parents had called, wondering why she hadn't been over.

She'd tell them about Hawaii tonight, Candy decided. Just get it over and done with and then maybe then she'd feel better. Yet she was incredibly tired and really just wanted to go home, have dinner and an early night.

'Here!'

That delicious voice tipped her out of introspection and she looked up at Steele, who was holding a stethoscope, which she took from him.

'Thank you,' Candy said, 'though you didn't have to rush to bring it back down. It's only a hospital-issue stethoscope.'

'Oh,' Steele said. 'I thought I'd pinched yours. Still, it doesn't matter, I was coming down anyway. I'm waiting for a patient to arrive—a direct admission from her GP, though she's refusing to go straight to the ward. She's just agreed to a chest X-ray and some blood tests, and then she thinks she's going home!'

'Thinks?' Candy asked as Steele sat down beside her and stretched out his long legs. It was nice that he sat down next to her when there were about twenty seats to choose from. She turned and smiled as he spoke on.

'Her GP is extremely concerned about her. He thinks there's far more going on than she's admitting to. Macey has had the same GP for thirty years and if he's worried about her then so am I. He thinks she's depressed.' He turned and looked right into her eyes and Candy felt her heart do a little flip-flop. 'It's a big problem with the elderly.'

'Really?'

Steele nodded and looked at what she was eating. 'That looks so bad it has to be good.'

'It's fantastic,' Candy said, and ripped off half her sandwich and gave it to him. 'The trick is lots of butter.'

'That's amazing!' Steele said, when he'd tasted it.

'I'm brilliant with bread,' Candy said. 'Toasted sandwiches, ice-cream sandwiches, beans on toast…'

'I thought a nice Italian girl like you would be brilliant in the kitchen.'

'Sadly, no,' Candy said. 'I'm a constant source of concern to my mother. Anyway, who said I'm nice?'

They smiled.

A smile that was just so deliciously inappropriate for a man you'd met only an hour or so ago. A smile she had never given to another man before and, really, she had no idea where it had come from.

Candy Anastasi! she scolded herself as she looked into those dark brown eyes.

Step away from the very young nurse, Steele told himself, but, hell, she was gorgeous.

Lydia came in then and they both looked away from each other. Lydia was waving a postcard of a delicious aqua ocean and Candy found that she was holding her breath in tension as Lydia read out the card. 'There's a postcard from Gerry. It reads, "Glad that none of you are here."'

Lydia gave a tight smile as she pinned it on the board and Candy just stared at the television.

Was that little dig from Gerry aimed at her?

'When is he back?' Trevor asked.

'End of July, I think.'

Lydia's voice was deliberately vague and Candy knew why. Gerry, the head nurse in Emergency, had been strongly advised to take extended leave.

Gerry was one of the reasons that Candy wanted a couple of weeks on a beach with no company.

Candy's parents had freaked when, at twenty-two, she had broken up with a man they considered suitable and had declared she was moving out. They had been so appalled, so devastated at the prospect of their only daughter leaving home that Candy had ended up staying for another year.

She'd simply had to leave in the end.

Her mother thought nothing of opening her post. She constantly asked whom Candy was talking to on the phone and when Candy pointed out she was entitled to privacy they would ask what it was she had to hide.

Last year she had moved out and, really, she had hardly let loose. She'd had a brief relationship with

Gerry when she'd first moved into her flat but that hadn't worked out and she had been happily single since then.

A couple of months ago, aware that Gerry was having some problems, she'd agreed to go out for a drink with him.

It had resulted in a one-night stand that had left Candy feeling regretful. Gerry had been annoyed to find out that their brief relationship hadn't been resumed.

It was all a bit of a mess, an avoidable one, though. Candy was just grateful that no one at work knew about that regrettable night and Candy wanted it left far behind.

'You'll be sending postcards soon,' Steele said, but Candy shook her head.

'I won't be thinking about this place for a moment.'

That wasn't quite true, though. She would be thinking about work—Candy was seriously thinking of leaving Emergency.

CHAPTER TWO

JUST AS SHE RETURNED from lunch she was informed that Steele's patient was here but refusing to come inside the department and had requested, loudly, that the ambulance take her home.

'I'll come out and have a word with her,' Candy said as Steele was taking a phone call. She headed out to the ambulance and was met by a teary woman who introduced herself as Catherine, Macey Anderson's niece.

'I knew that she was going to do this,' Catherine said. 'It's taken two days to persuade her to come in. She used to be a matron on one of the wards here, and still thinks she is one.' Catherine gave a tired smile. 'She was in a few months ago and she was just about running the place by the time she was discharged.'

'I want to go home,' Macey shouted as Candy came into the back of the ambulance.

Macey was a very tall, very handsome woman, with wiry grey, curly hair, a flushed face and very angry dark green eyes. She had all her stuff with her, a huge suitcase, a walking frame and several other bags.

'Mrs Anderson—' Candy started, but already she was wrong.

'It's Miss Anderson!'

'I'm sorry, Miss Anderson. I'm Candy Anastasi, one of the nurses in Emergency, and I'm going to be looking after you today.'

'But, as I've told everyone, many times, I don't *want* to be looked after,' Macey retorted. 'I want to be taken home.'

It was all pretty hopeless. The more they tried to persuade her to come into the department the more upset Macey became. The last thing Candy wanted to do was wheel her through when she was distressed and crying and so, instead, she tried another tack, wondering if, given that Macey had once been a matron, she might not want to get another nurse in trouble.

'Dr Steele is already here to see you,' Candy said. 'He's been waiting for you to arrive. Am I to go in and tell him that I can't get you to come into the hospital?'

Macey looked at her for a long moment and then she looked beyond Candy's shoulder and Candy knew, she simply knew, that it was Steele who had just stepped into the ambulance.

'Is there a problem, Nurse? Only I've been waiting for quite some time.' His low voice sounded just a touch ominous and Candy met Macey's eyes for a brief moment.

'No,' Macey answered for Candy. 'They were just about to bring me in.'

'Good,' Steele said. 'Then I'll come and see you shortly, Miss Anderson.'

As he headed back into the department the paramedics lowered the stretcher to the ground and Candy found out perhaps why it was that Steele was so sharply dressed. 'At least he's not twelve and wearing jeans,' Macey muttered.

Candy smiled—yes, Steele's appearance and authoritarian tone had appeased Macey.

They took Macey into cubicle seven, aligned the stretcher with the trolley, and Candy positioned the sliding board that would help to move the patient over easily. 'We'll get you onto the trolley, Miss Anderson.'

'I can manage,' the elderly lady snapped, 'and it's Macey.'

'That actually means she likes you,' her niece said, and gestured with her head for Candy to follow her outside.

'I've got this,' Matthew, a very patient paramedic, said, and Candy went outside to speak with Catherine.

'It's taken two days for her GP to persuade her to come in,' Catherine said. 'Honestly, I'm just so relieved she's finally here. She's got a temperature and she's hardly eating or drinking anything. She doesn't take her tablets or if she does she gets them all wrong...'

'We'll go through all of that.' Candy did her best to reassure Macey's niece.

'She's so cantankerous and rude,' Catherine said, 'that she puts everyone offside, but she's such a lovely lady too. She's always been on her own, she's never had a boyfriend, let alone married, she's so completely set in her ways and loathes getting undressed in front of anyone. You're going to have a battle there...'

'Let us take care of her,' Candy said, 'and please don't worry about her saying something offensive. Believe me, we'll have heard far worse.'

'Thanks.' Catherine gave a worried smile and they went back inside. The cubicle was pretty full, with Macey's huge bag and walking frame, and Candy had

a little tidy up. 'Why don't we first get you into a gown
and then—'

'Get me into a gown?' Macey shouted loudly. 'You
haven't even introduced yourself and you're asking me
to take my clothes off.' Candy said nothing as Steele
came into the cubicle. She had, in fact, introduced herself in the ambulance. 'You're not a nurse's bootlace,'
Macey said to Candy just as Steele came in.

'Hello, Miss Anderson,' he said. 'I didn't introduce
myself properly back there in the ambulance. I'm
Steele, or Dr Steele, if you prefer to be formal.'

Candy smothered a little smile as he repeated a sim-
ilar introduction to the one he had given her. He must
have to say it fifty times a day.

He ran through a few questions with Macey as a
very anxious Catherine hovered.

'You had a heart attack three months ago?' Steele
checked. 'And you were admitted here for a week.'

'All they did was pump me with drugs,' Macey
huffed. 'Where were you then?'

'I believe I was in Newcastle,' Steele said.

'So how long have you worked here?'

'Two days,' Steele answered easily.

'You'll be gone tomorrow.' Macey huffed. 'You're
a locum.'

'I am, though I happen to be a very good one,' Steele
said, completely unfazed. 'And I'm here for six weeks,
which gives us plenty of time to sort all this out.'

They went through her medical history. Apart from
the heart attack it would seem that Macey was very
well indeed. She had never smoked, never drunk, and
at eighty still did all her own housework and cooking, with a little help from her nieces, Catherine and

Linda. Macey had until a couple of days ago walked to the shops every day.

'It's quite a distance,' Catherine said. 'I offered to do her shopping weekly at the supermarket for her but Aunt Macey wouldn't hear of it.'

'I like to walk,' Macey snapped.

'It's good that you do—exercise is good for you,' Steele said. 'Do you have stairs at home?'

'Yes, and I manage them just fine,' Macey retorted. 'You won't see me with bungalow legs!'

'Right, Miss Anderson,' Steele said. 'I'm going to ask Candy to help you into a gown and do some obs and put an IV and draw some blood. Then I'll come and examine you.' He looked at two blue ice-cream containers that were filled with various bottles and blister packets of medication. 'I'll take these and look through them.'

As Steele went to go Macey called him back. 'I'm not having a nurse take my blood. That's a doctor's job.'

'Oh, I can assure you that you're better off with Candy than you are with me,' Steele said. 'I get the shakes this side of six p.m.'

His quip caused a little smile to inch onto Macey's lips and, after Steele had gone, Candy helped her into a gown while doing her best to keep Macey covered as she did so. But the elderly lady fought her over every piece, right down to her stockings.

'Leave my stockings on,' Macey said.

'Oh, I'll leave them for Steele to take off, shall I?' Candy challenged.

Macey huffed and lifted her bottom but as Candy rolled the stockings down she found out why Macey was so reluctant to get fully undressed—there was a bandage on her leg and around that the skin was very red and inflamed.

'I'll take this off so Steele can take a look,' Candy said. She went and washed her hands and opened up a dressing pack and then put on some gloves.

'Careful,' Macey warned.

'Is it very painful?' Candy asked, and Macey nodded.

'Okay, I'll just put some saline on,' Candy said, 'and we'll soak it off. Has your GP seen this?'

'I don't need a doctor to tell me how to do a dressing.'

Candy soaked the dressing in saline and then covered Macey with a blanket and checked her obs, before heading out to Steele. He was sitting at the nurses' station, going through all Macey's medications. He had a pill counter and was tipping one of the bottles out when Candy came over.

'She's got a nasty leg wound,' Candy said.

'How bad?'

'I haven't seen it,' Candy said. 'I'm just soaking the dressing but her shin is all red and I think it's very painful.'

'Okay.' He started to tip the tablets back into the jar. 'I don't want her left on her own,' Steele said.

'Sorry?'

'I don't like what I'm seeing with these tablets,' Steele said. 'I don't trust her not to do something stupid.'

'Oh!'

'I'll come in and see her now.'

They both returned to the cubicle and Steele examined Macey. He listened for a long time to her chest and felt her stomach, keeping her as covered as he could while he did so, and then they got to her leg.

Steele put on some gloves and took off the dressing and Macey winced in pain. 'Sorry, Miss Anderson,' Steele said. 'How long have you had this?'

'A couple of weeks.'

Steele looked up at Macey. 'That's very concerning. This has developed over two weeks?'

Candy could hear the note of sarcasm in Steele's voice and watched as Macey stared back at him and then backed down.

'I knocked my leg when I came out of hospital. It's just not healed and it's been getting worse.'

'That sounds far more plausible.' Steele smiled at her. 'Well, that accounts for your temperature!' He took a swab and though he was very gentle the cotton tip must have felt like a red-hot poker because Macey let out a yelp of pain. 'Very sorry, Macey,' Steele said. He put a light dressing over it. 'We'll give you something decent for pain before we dress it properly.' He spoke then to Candy. 'Can you take Macey round for a chest X-ray?'

Just as Candy had finished drawing some blood the porter arrived and Candy went to X-Ray with Macey and Catherine. They were seen relatively quickly but Macey was clearly less than impressed at what she considered a long wait.

Having looked at her X-ray, Steele came into the cubicle and then turned to Catherine. 'Why don't you go and get a drink?' he suggested. 'I'm going to be with your aunt for the next twenty minutes or so—you might as well take the chance for a break now.'

'Thank you,' Catherine said in relief.

'I just wanted to check a couple of things,' Steele said once Catherine had left the cubicle.

'And then I can go home?'

'You're not well enough,' Steele said. 'Now, while Catherine isn't here, I want you to tell me how many you smoke a day?'

'I don't smoke.'

'Miss Anderson, do you want me to bring in your chest X-ray and we can go over it together?'

'Two.' She gave a tight shrug. 'Maybe three a day.'

'We'll say ten, then, shall we?' Steele said, and Candy blinked when Macey didn't correct him. 'I'll write you up for a nicotine patch. How much do you drink a day?'

'I've told you already, I don't.'

'Six broken ribs of varying ages.' Steele smiled at the old girl. 'Come on, Macey. So am I to worry that you're falling down for no reason?'

'I slipped on some ice,' Macey said, 'and I've got a cat that gets under my feet.'

'Fair enough.' Steele nodded. 'So you don't want me to write you down for a couple of shots of sherry at night?' he checked. 'You can have either your own stuff, or the hospital's cheap disgusting stuff. We just need the bottle if you want to drink your own.'

Macey took in a deep breath before saying anything. 'It's in my bag.'

'Good, we'll make sure it's handed over to nursing staff out of sight of your niece.'

Candy stood there feeling a bit stunned but she hadn't seen anything yet. Steele had brought back in the two ice-cream containers that Macey had brought in with her and he started to go through them.

'Macey, you haven't been taking these regularly.' He held up a pill bottle. 'Yet you're not.'

'There's so many. I can't keep up.'

Steele picked up another bottle that had just a couple of tablets in it. 'And these were only dispensed two days ago,' Steele said, 'and there are only two left.'

'I didn't take them,' Macey said in a scoffing voice.

'I know that you didn't or we wouldn't even be having this conversation. So where are they now?'

'I don't know. My niece puts them into a pill box…'

'Macey?'

'I tipped them down the toilet. I don't trust the drug companies.'

'Are you depressed, Macey?'

'Oh, you're going to put me on antidepressants now. You're in cahoots with the drug companies.'

'Are you confused and mixing up your medication or are you ignoring your health?' Steele asked, and Candy stood there, watching him stare right into Macey's eyes. 'Are you depressed, Macey?'

There was a long stretch of silence before Macey answered.

'I'm not confused,' she said. 'Well, sometimes I am with dates and things.'

'But you're not confused where your medication's concerned?' Steele checked.

'No,' Macey said, and Candy frowned at the serious note to Steele's voice.

'Okay.'

'Could you just leave me, please?' Macey asked.

'Not happening,' Steele said, and he took down the edge of the trolley she was lying on. His legs were long enough that he sat there easily. She would need a ladder to do that, Candy thought, and then she stopped thinking idle thoughts as she started to realise the seriousness of this conversation.

'Why did you tip the tablets in the toilet?' Steele challenged gently, and Candy felt the back of her nose stinging as he pushed on. 'Were you scared that you might take them all?'

Macey's face started to crumple and Steele took her hand. 'Look at me, Macey. Are you having suicidal thoughts?' Steele asked bluntly, and after a moment she nodded and then started to cry.

'Well done for throwing them away,' Steele said. 'Well done for coming into hospital and speaking with me.' Candy watched as he wrapped his arms around the proud lady as she started to really sob. 'It's okay.' His voice was very deep but so gentle. 'We're going to look after you...'

CHAPTER THREE

CANDY SLEPT FOR a few hours on Friday afternoon before her first night shift on the geriatric ward and then she got ready and took the Underground into work.

She was actually rather nervous about her night shift. She was so used to working in Emergency that she wasn't too sure how she would go on the ward. She also had a short four-hour shift there on Sunday morning.

It will be worth it, Candy told herself as she stepped into the geriatric unit.

Hawaii, here I come!

The handover lasted much longer than it did in Emergency and the day staff went into far more detail about the patients than she had grown used to. Candy sat as the staff discussed in depth the patients' moods and their ADLs: activities of daily living. Steele was sitting at a desk in the room with his back to everyone but didn't leave as the handover started; he just carried on with whatever he was doing on the computer and offered comment or clarification at times.

Candy knew that she was far, far too aware of him.

The staff clearly liked him. If there was a question

they would toss it over to him and he would answer as he typed away.

Elaine, a student nurse, was giving her handover to the night staff, watched over by her mentor, Gloria. Elaine was very bossy and seemed to think she was the only one in the room who knew what she was doing. She had given a sigh of exasperation when Candy had introduced herself and said that she was from the hospital bank. 'Another one!' Elaine had said.

As Elaine gave her handover there were a few times when Candy caught Abigail's eye—Abigail was the senior nurse she would be working with tonight, and they both smothered a smile.

Mr Heath, who had been so unwell the other day in Emergency, was doing a lot better and Candy was allocated to look after him for the night.

She was also given Toby Worthington, a terminal patient who was on a lot of morphine for pain control and, Elaine said, liked to have his radio on till eleven at night and then turned on again at six.

'Then we have Macey Anderson.' Elaine moved on to the next patient.

'I know Macey,' Candy said. 'I was in Emergency when she was admitted.'

'Could you have her tonight as well, then?' Abigail checked and Candy nodded. They went through her history, which was pretty much what Candy already knew. How Macey had been since admission had changed rapidly, though. 'Since she's come to the ward she's been very withdrawn,' Elaine said. 'She doesn't want to eat, or wash. She's on an IV regime but if she continues to refuse meals and drinks she'll need an NG tube. Steele has taken her off a lot of her medications and has also started her on a low dose of antidepressants…' Elaine went through her medications. 'Make sure she takes them and she's not hiding them,' Elaine warned, and Candy nodded. But that wasn't enough for Elaine. 'You have to ask her to lift her tongue.'

'I shall,' Candy said, trying to keep the edge from her voice. Elaine was a funny little thing, with a very long, wide mouth that opened often.

She reminded Candy of a puppet.

'Why does she have to lift her tongue, Elaine?' Steele asked from the computer, and Candy felt her lips stretch into a smile because clearly he had Elaine worked out too.

'To make sure that she's not hiding any under there,' Elaine said, and looked at Candy to make sure that she understood the instruction.

'Thanks,' Candy said. 'I'll make sure that she takes them.'

As Elaine left the room Abigail winked. 'Matron Elaine!'

'Her heart's in the right place, though,' Gloria, the sister in charge of the day shift, said. 'But, oh my, she's hard work. Elaine insists on calling everything by its technical name. The patients haven't a clue what she's asking. Just this evening she asked Mr Heath if she could check for scrotal oedema.' Gloria smiled as she recalled it. 'He said, "Do you mean my balls, dear?" It was too funny.'

They were all very nice and after handover Elaine gave Candy a quick tour of the ward before she headed for home.

Actually, it wasn't that quick—Elaine was incredibly thorough, going through everything in detail when really Candy wanted to get started.

'I think that covers everything,' Candy said. 'Thanks for the tour.'

'I'll just show you where the torches and things are kept,' Elaine said, but Candy looked at the clock and it was already nearly ten. 'Go.' Candy smiled. 'It's Friday night. Enjoy it!'

Elaine gave a little nod and finally headed for home and then Candy went to check on her patients for the night.

Mr Heath was indeed looking better.

'Hello, Candy.' He smiled when she came over and he put down the book that he was reading.

'You remember me?' Candy asked in surprise, because Mr Heath had been so distressed in Resus that he hadn't seemed very aware of his surroundings or able to hear what anybody except Steele was saying.

'Of course I do.'

'Well, it's lovely to see you looking so much better,' Candy said. She then did his obs and gave him his medications for the night and, as she did so, they chatted for a while.

'I'm hoping to go home on Monday,' Mr Heath said. 'My granddaughter gets married next week.'

'How exciting,' Candy said. 'Is it a big wedding?'

'Huge!' Mr Heath nodded. 'She's marrying an Ital...' His voice trailed off.

'Don't stop on my account.' Candy grinned. 'I know what Italian weddings can be like. I must be the only girl in the world who's dreaded her wedding day since she was little rather than dreamt of it.'

Mr Heath laughed. 'Will it be big?'

'You have no idea,' Candy said. 'I have four older brothers, all married, and my mother is itching for it to be my turn. She buys sheets and towels for me when she shops—oh, and washing baskets and the like. I'm all set up!' Candy smiled. 'Apart from the groom.'

It was, in fact, a very friendly ward and the staff didn't mind that Candy had a few questions every now and then. But as she went to do Macey's medications, Candy frowned and looked around for Abigail, but she was in with Mrs Douglas, who was very sick indeed.

'Problem?' Steele had come onto the ward and was writing up some medication for a patient who wasn't Candy's.

'No, I just want to check something,' Candy said, taking the prescription chart over to him. 'Macey's written up for sherry, but she's on a lot of other medication.'

'No doubt she'll be having the sherry when she gets home,' Steele pointed out. 'Though I don't think you have to worry about it tonight—she's not having her sherry at the moment. She's not really having much of anything.'

He was right. Candy was shocked at the change in Macey. She'd been a fierce, proud woman when she had arrived in the emergency department but now she just lay on her side and stared into space. She didn't say anything when Candy introduced herself and her arm was listless when Candy checked her blood pressure.

'I've got your tablets for you, Macey,' Candy explained, and she helped her to sit up to take them. The old lady took her tablets without a word of protest and then tried to take the water Candy offered, but her hands were shaking terribly so Candy held the glass and helped her take a drink to wash them down. 'Sorry, Macey, but can you lift your tongue for me?'

She lifted her tongue and, yes, she had swallowed all the tablets rather than hiding them. Then she lay back down on the pillow.

'Can I get you anything else?' Candy offered. 'A drink?'

Macey gave a small shake of her head and Candy looked at the fluid balance and food charts. She was on an IV, and that was, apart from the water she took with her medicines, practically all that Macey was having at the moment.

'Macey,' Candy suggested as she put another blanket on and turned her pillows, 'why don't I get you some milk?'

Her lethargy was troubling. Candy would far prefer her to be shouting at her and telling her that she wasn't a nurse's bootlace.

'Some warm milk,' Candy elaborated. 'I know your hands are a bit shaky at the moment but I can help you to drink it. Will you have some milk?'

Macey didn't say yes but at least she didn't shake her head this time.

Steele looked over and saw Candy hovering, sorting out pillows and blankets on Macey's bed. He half expected Macey to shout for her to get off as she had done when she'd been with the other nurse that afternoon, but he was pleased to see that tonight Macey didn't seem to mind the small attention.

Steele liked Candy, which had certainly come as a surprise to him.

The attraction had been instant, yet Candy was nothing like the women Steele usually dated.

Oh, he dated.

A lot.

Steele went for sophisticated women. He liked women who understood right from the start that this could only ever be a fleeting thing for he was never anywhere long. Six months here, two years there and now just six weeks here.

Steele glanced at the date. He had been here almost a week, so make that five weeks he had left at the Royal.

And Candy was away for the final two of them.

Steele had already done the marriage-and-settle-down thing and it hadn't worked.

Or rather, it had worked, possibly more than he had realised, because ten years on his ex-wife, completely out of the blue, had rung him. Her second marriage had failed and she had suggested that they give it another go. Even before Steele could answer her and say he had never heard a more ridiculous suggestion in his life she had added her little postscript—there was one proviso to them getting back together.

There had been a lot of advances in technology after all.

Ten years on the hurt was there and she had just hit it with a sledgehammer again. His one raw nerve, the one chink in his confident persona, had been exposed again. Steele had promptly hung up on her without response because otherwise he might well have exploded and told her exactly the words that were in his head.

They weren't pretty.

For Steele, finding out that he was infertile had been a huge blow. His wife's response to the news had been devastating.

He made sure now he was never in a position to

reveal that part of himself again. He kept things light; he kept things intimate sexually rather than emotionally.

Then he moved on.

Candy walked past just then, carrying a feeding cup, and she went over and helped Macey to sit up.

Candy didn't say anything; she just gave Macey a smile as the elderly lady took sips of the milky drink. That was all Macey wanted for now: no conversation, just a warm drink and the comfort of companionable silence.

Candy was fine with that—she was used to it, in fact.

When she'd been ten, her *nonna* had come to live with them. Candy's job in the morning had been to make sure Nonna got her *biscotti* and milky coffee and then to see her to the bathroom and make up her bed. Candy had loved the mornings—the chatty ones when Nonna had told her all about the village that she had grown up in. The reminiscent ones when Nonna had spoken about falling in love and the parties and dancing. The sad ones—leaving Italy and the death of her husband, Candy's *nonno*. Candy had been comfortable too with the silent mornings, when Nonna had just eaten quietly, lost in a world of her own, as Macey was now.

'Do you want a bedpan?' Candy offered Macey when the milk was gone.

'I'll go...' Macey sighed and pulled back the bed covers.

Glad to see that she was making the effort to get out of bed, Candy helped her with her slippers and got Macey her walking frame and they walked over to the bathroom.

Candy waited outside and when Macey came to wash her hands Candy sorted the taps and squeezed the soap for her. Macey washed her hands very thoroughly. Her nail varnish was chipped and Candy watched her examine her nails for a moment, clearly less than impressed with the state of her hands.

'I'll sort your nails out for you on Sunday,' Candy offered, and then took Macey back to her bedside, where she asked her to sit for a moment. 'Sit there and let me make it up all nice and fresh for you to get into.'

Candy made the bed so nicely that she wanted to climb in it herself. 'You'd better get in quickly or I will.'

'You look tired,' Macey said, and Candy smiled at the first invitation to conversation.

'I am, though I shouldn't be,' Candy said. 'I slept all afternoon.'

She got the older woman into bed, put up the bed rails and tied the call bell to the side. 'Press it if you need anything,' Candy said. 'I hope you have a lovely sleep.'

Candy sorted out her other patients and, by one a.m., when Abigail asked if she'd mind taking the first break, Candy was more than ready for an hour to rest. It would seem she wasn't the only one who needed a doze, because when she walked into the break room there was Steele, asleep on a sofa with the television on in the background.

'Aloha,' he said sleepily, when Candy disturbed him as she took a seat.

'Aloha.' Candy smiled. 'How come you're still here?'

'I'm waiting for some relatives to come in for Mrs Douglas.'

Candy remembered from handover that Mrs Douglas wasn't expected to make it through the night.

'How long is it now till your holiday?' Steele asked.

'Three weeks,' Candy said, and set her phone alarm for an hour's time. She saw the date and that it was now Saturday morning. 'Actually, just under three weeks. I fly on a Friday night.'

'Are you working right up till then?'

Candy nodded and then yawned at the very thought. 'I almost go from here to the airport.'

'Is it just you going?'

'Yep.'

'I thought Hawaii was more a couples' destination,' Steele said, fishing shamelessly.

'I think you may be right but I saw an advert and I couldn't resist,' Candy admitted and nodded to the television, where an infomercial for knives was showing. 'It was a limited offer, with a huge discount for the first ten to call... I fall for it every time'

'Yep.' Steele nodded. 'And me. I bought the juicer, the chopper and some blender thing until I finally worked out that nothing is going to make me like vegetables.'

'It's one of the perils of working nights,' Candy agreed. 'What looks appealing at two a.m. seems stupid when the parcel arrives. Anyway, I saw the advert for the holiday when I was feeling particularly miserable. It looked absolutely beautiful and I really needed to get away...'

'How come?'

'Lots of things really.'

'Such as?'

Candy hesitated. She hadn't really spoken to anyone about the fact she was considering leaving. She glanced at Steele and realised that by the time she got back from Hawaii he'd be gone, so it really made no difference. 'I'm not sure if I still want to work in Emergency.'

'It must be a pretty stressful job.'

'It is at times.' Candy nodded. 'Though it's not just that. I made a mistake couple of months back.' She didn't elaborate; instead, she lay down on the sofa, determined to squeeze in some sleep during her break.

'A professional mistake?' Steele probed, and Candy let out a small laugh at his very direct question.

'No, it was a personal one.'

'Do tell.'

'No way.'

'So there are two things I have to find out about you now,' Steele teased. 'The story behind your name and the mistake that Nurse Candy made.'

'You can try, but it won't get you anywhere,' Candy said, and closed her eyes. 'I'm going to have a little rest.'

'Hopefully you talk in your sleep.'

She smiled with her eyes closed and was mildly surprised when after a moment or so Steele continued to speak.

'We all make mistakes, Candy,' he said. His lovely deep voice was soothing and broke into her semi-doze. 'If I've learnt one thing in this job, it's that everyone makes so-called mistakes and also that everyone wastes way too much time regretting them.'

She opened her eyes and looked at him. 'You really

do like your job,' Candy said, and it wasn't a question, more an observation, and Steele nodded.

'I really do.'

Yes, she should sleep and her aching body might regret it later but she chose to forgo the full hour of sleep just to find out a little more about him. She lay there and peeked over to Steele, who was still looking at her.

'Did you always want to work in geriatrics?'

'Not really,' Steele said. 'It sort of found me, I guess. I was pretty much raised by my grandmother…'

'Are your parents…?' Her voice trailed off and Steele grinned.

'They're not dead.'

'Good.'

'My parents are both doctors and were very serious about their careers. I was a late accident. I don't think they ever really wanted to have children. My mother was a top thoracic surgeon—which means she had balls.'

Candy laughed.

'My grandmother looked after me till I went to boarding school and in the holidays I stayed with her.' He saw her frown. 'My parents are good people. They were just very, very focused. Anyway, when I went to my grandmother's for Easter one year, she was very confused. Just completely off the wall. I rang my mother and she pretty much would have had her shipped off to a nursing home that day.'

'Really?' Candy said.

'Really!' Steele nodded. 'But the GP came and it turned out all she had was a urine infection. He explained the confusion it could cause in the elderly. Anyway, two days later she was completely back to herself. It just stayed with me, I guess.'

'My *nonna* lived with us.' Candy yawned. 'I think my mother thinks she'll be living with me...'

'Did your mother work?' Steele asked, and Candy shook her head. 'You do, though. You have a career.'

Candy looked at him. Right there, right then, she felt as if he knew the wrestle in her heart because though she loved her parents they clashed a lot as Candy struggled to be independent when they didn't want her to be. 'I do have a career,' Candy said, 'and I had to fight to have one.'

'Have your rest.' He smiled and Candy nodded.

She'd had to fight to simply be here, Candy thought as she closed her eyes. Her parents had wanted her to marry Franco, and for her to work in the family business. They hadn't understood that she'd wanted to study to become a nurse.

Candy fell asleep but it felt about twenty seconds later that her phone bleeped and told her that her hour was up and it was time to go back to work. The staff-room was empty and when she went round to the ward Steele wasn't there either.

She liked him.

Candy knew it properly then because she preferred the feel on the ward when he was around.

The rest of the night flew past quickly. Candy helped out with Mrs Douglas while Abigail took her break and then it was time to start her morning routine. At seven-thirty, after handover, Candy said goodbye to her patients and told Macey that she would be in to-morrow morning and, if Macey liked and Candy had time, then she would do her nails.

Macey said nothing.

As Candy walked along the main entrance corridor she saw Steele on his way into work. His hair was damp from his morning shower and he was wearing a dark grey suit and fresh shirt, though he hadn't yet done up his tie. He was standing looking at one of the pictures that lined the corridor, images of the hospital and the changes over the years. Renovations were taking place throughout the Royal.

'What are you looking at?' she asked.

'Come and see,' Steele invited, and as she stood beside him he started to do up his tie. 'Do you recognise anyone?'

Candy peered at the image that he had been focused on. It was a group of nurses and doctors standing in the gardens at the rear of the hospital. It looked like a presentation had just taken place as some of the nurses were sporting medals. Candy smiled when she saw the long dresses and aprons that the nurses were wearing as well as their hats and capes. Then she saw just who it was that Steele was looking at. 'Oh, my goodness, it's Macey.'

'It is indeed.'

She had the same wild curly hair, though it was tamed by a frilly white cap. Her cheekbones were high and her lips, though smiling, looked a touch strained. Her cape was around her shoulders and Candy smiled at the red cross that it made on her chest.

She looked incredibly young but certainly it was Macey.

'Do you think she'll come out of her depression?' Candy asked.

'Now I do.'

'What do you mean?'

But Steele didn't answer her directly. 'You were very good with her last night. I'm glad she had a drink and got up to the bathroom. How was she this morning?'

'Still very quiet, but she had another drink and I made her *biscotti*, which she ate.'

'*Biscotti?*'

'Biscuits in warm milk, all mashed in.' Candy smiled and then groaned as her stomach rumbled just at the thought. 'Now I've gone and made myself hungry, I'll have to have some when I get home.'

'Did you feed her?'

'I did.' Candy nodded. 'She's very shaky.'

'It's all the new medications,' Steele said, 'and a lack of sherry, but it should soon start to settle down.'

'How did you know that she was drinking?'

'Because drinking is incredibly common in the elderly. Far more than people realise. It's not all bad.' Steele smiled. 'Macey can't ask her niece to get her four bottles of sherry a week, or however much it is that she actually drinks. At least it keeps her walking to the shops each day. I admit that I worry what will happen when my oldies all discover online shopping.'

Candy realised she was doing her dental commercial smile at him again.

He made her smile.

'I'm going home.' Candy hitched up her bag. 'I'll say goodnight because it's night-time to me.'

'Have a good sleep,' Steele said, 'and don't talk too much.'

'I *don't* talk in my sleep.' She smiled back at him. 'At least, I don't think I do.'

As she walked off his deep voice caused her shoulders to stiffen.

'Make that three things that I have to find out about you.'

Oh, my God, Candy realised.

They *were* flirting.

More than that, she was considering revising her recently put in place rule—to never again get involved with someone at work.

He was *that* good.

CHAPTER FOUR

'CAN I HAVE a hand to turn Mr Worthington, please?' Candy asked Elaine the following morning.

She had slept all of Saturday and had then got up for dinner and gone out for a couple of hours with Kelly, only to be in bed by ten and asleep again in a matter of moments.

And she was *still* tired.

Elaine was very brusque and efficient and they soon had Mr Worthington turned. 'Why isn't his radio on?' Elaine asked, turning it on. 'Toby likes to have his radio on, especially on a Sunday morning. I wrote it down in his care plan.'

'Sorry,' Candy muttered as Elaine marched out.

As bossy as she was, though, Elaine's heart really was in the right place because Toby started humming a little as Candy shaved him and all too soon she found herself singing along to the Sunday morning hymns. It made Toby smile and his eyes encouraged her and he even started singing along to some of the choruses, which only made Candy sing louder.

'Mr Worthington!' Gloria popped her head in. 'Your family are here to see you.' She smiled at Candy.

'They'll be pleased to see him looking so cheerful. Steele was just having a word with them.'

Candy quickly tidied up the room and moved the trolley out of the way as Toby's family thanked Steele and then smiled at Candy as they made their way in.

'Did you enjoy your little singalong?' Steele asked when she came out.

'Actually, I did,' she said, 'although I'm not sure quite what Toby would have to say about it if he was able to talk.'

'Oh, I'm sure that, with the amount of morphine he's on, your voice sounded pretty fantastic.'

'Are you telling me that I'm tone deaf?'

'Ooh, just a touch,' Steele teased, but it didn't faze Candy.

'I'm going to sing louder next time.'

They would have chatted for longer but Matron Elaine was back and ready to move things along. 'Come on, Candy, we're falling behind. I'll help you with Macey.'

Candy would really prefer that she didn't.

'Have fun!' Steele said as Candy rolled her eyes.

The strangest thing was, though, that Candy did enjoy herself.

In fact, she had more fun then she'd had in a long time and so did Macey!

'Good morning, Macey.' Candy smiled as she pulled the curtains around the bed. 'Would you like to have a shower?'

Macey gave a slow shake of her head.

'Well, Elaine and I will give you a wash in bed, if that's okay, and we'll give you some nice fresh sheets and things. Then I'll do your leg dressing.'

'I'll do Macey's leg dressing,' Elaine said. 'I need to practice my aseptic technique.'

'Sure,' Candy agreed, and then spoke to Macey. 'Would you like me to wash your hair? We can do it in bed. I just need to take the bedhead off. It might make you feel a little bit better,' Candy pushed gently, but again Macey shook her head.

Elaine had everything set up on the trolley to wash Macey and she was busy collecting sheets and pillow-cases for the bed change as Candy washed Macey's face. She then offered her the cloth to wash her hands but Macey didn't take it so Candy washed Macey's hands in the bowl. 'I'll take that nail varnish off in a little while and do your nails.'

'There isn't time to do nails,' Elaine said as she returned.

'I'll do it on my coffee break,' Candy said as they turned Macey and washed her back. Elaine was starting to seriously get on her nerves. 'I like painting nails.'

Delightfully, though, as Macey was turned back from her side she caught Candy's eye and gave her a tiny wink. This showed Candy she was coming back to the world and that Macey understood how difficult Elaine might be to work with.

She returned the wink and soaped up the cloth again.

'Would you like to wash yourself down there?' Candy offered, so that Macey could wash her private parts herself, but both Candy and Macey blinked at the same time when a loud voice interrupted them.

'No!' Elaine said. 'We do not speak down to our patients. You are to call it by its proper name.'

Candy shared a brief *yikes* look with Macey.

'I apologise, Macey,' she said, looking into Macey's eyes as they both tried to fathom what it was that she was supposed to say.

'Would you like to wash your private parts?' Candy offered and saw Macey's lips start to twitch into a smile, especially when Elaine chimed up again.

'No!' she said. 'You're to call it by its proper name.'

Given that Candy was the qualified nurse, she could have told Elaine to simply be quiet, but there was a glimmer in Macey's eyes that hadn't been there for a long time and, Candy guessed as they shared a smile, she was more than happy for the exchange to continue.

Macey presumably had a nurse's sense of humour after all.

'I'm sorry, Macey,' Candy said again as she stretched her brain as to what she should say. She rinsed out the cloth again and then mouthed to Macey, 'What do I say?'

Macey offered a tiny shrug.

Was she supposed to ask if she wanted to wash her vagina? 'Macey,' Candy said, and cleared her throat. They stared seriously at each other, though they were both laughing on the inside. Each knew the other's thoughts. 'Would you like to wash your genitals?'

'No!' Elaine, clearly incensed by Candy's apparent ineptitude, took the cloth from Candy. 'This is how you do it,' Elaine said, and soaped up the cloth again. 'Macey,' she said, holding out the cloth, 'would you like to wash your muffy?'

Macey and Candy cried from laughing.

Not in front of Elaine, of course, but as Elaine went to set up for the leg dressing Candy had to wipe the tears from Macey's eyes as they tried to keep their laughter quiet.

They clearly didn't succeed because Steele popped his head in.

'Did Elaine do her muffy thing again?' he asked.

'She did.' Candy grinned. 'Has she done it before, then?'

Steele nodded. 'Somebody has to tell her that that's not the technical name for it.' Steele grinned. 'Please, God, it's not me.'

'She'll be a wonderful nurse,' Macey said, still smiling. 'At least she's thorough.'

Candy was told to go for her coffee break and so she made a mug of coffee and put it beside Macey's bed, ready to set to work on her nails.

'Have your break,' Macey said.

'I honestly like painting nails,' Candy said. 'I do my mum's every week and I just wish I had four sisters instead of four brothers. It really does relax me.'

She held up a bottle of coral nail polish. 'Is that colour okay?'

Macey gave a small nod.

Macey sat quietly as Candy set to work. Candy didn't chat very much because she really was concentrating. There was something so soothing about painting nails that she truly did enjoy doing it. The immediate improvement was instantly gratifying and having nice nails was also a very easy lift to the sprits.

'Four brothers?' Macey said suddenly.

'And then came a daughter.' Candy gave a wry smile.

'Are they very strict?'

'They are but they're also very lovely. I know that

I really have nothing to complain about, but…' Candy shook her head. 'I'm still plucking up the courage to tell them that I've booked a holiday to Hawaii. They're not going to be pleased.'

'Why?' Macey asked. 'Because you're going with your boyfriend?'

'I don't have a boyfriend,' Candy said, taking Macey's other hand and starting to work on those nails. 'That won't appease them, though…me in America on my own…'

Macey looked across the ward and saw that Steele was looking towards them, or rather at Candy. When he realised that she was watching him he gave her a very brief smile and then looked away.

She might not say much but Macey knew everything that went on in the ward.

'There,' Candy said, finishing off and admiring her handiwork. 'Let them dry for a little while before you do anything.'

'No washing my muffy for the next half-hour, then,' Macey joked and smiled at Candy as she rested her head back on the pillow. 'Thank you, my dear.'

As she went to take her mug through to the kitchen Candy passed Steele. 'What time do you finish?' he asked.

'Eleven-thirty,' Candy said.

'Do you want to get lunch?'

He'd completely sideswiped her but, then, Candy thought, he had been doing that since the moment she'd clapped eyes on him. 'The canteen?' she suggested.

'If you like but I think we can do better than the canteen.'

Oh!

Did she want to have lunch with the sexiest man she had ever met? There really wasn't an awful lot to think about.

'Yes,' Candy said, 'that sounds great.'

'Good.'

'But aren't you on call?'

'My registrar can earn his keep for a couple of hours,' Steele said.

Wow.

There really was no messing with Steele; she had never really known anyone as direct as him before.

'Anyway,' Steele added, 'I've got a few questions that I'd like to know the answers to.'

'Question one,' Steele said as they sat in a very nice café that was just a short drive from the hospital. 'I want to know about your name—Candy?'

'You'll never know,' Candy said as she looked through the menu. 'It's the reason I'm never getting married. It's the reason I'm going on holiday alone. No one is allowed to see my passport!'

'I'm determined to find out.'

'You can be as determined as you like.' She smiled. 'It doesn't mean that you'll get anywhere, though.'

'What do you want to eat?' Steele asked.

'I would like…' She looked through the menu. What would she like? 'I fancy a roast.'

'Have a roast, then.'

'I shall.' Candy nodded. 'A Sunday roast is exotic to me. It was pasta and pasta and more pasta when I was growing up.'

'Well, I'll have the pasta, then.' He smiled, glad to

be out with someone who seemed to enjoy their food. 'That's exotic to me.'

'Please.' Candy rolled her eyes.

'Okay, second question—what was the mistake?'

Candy let out a breath; if this was leading anywhere, and it felt as if it was, then possibly she ought to tell him. Or possibly not, given that Steele would be long since gone by the time Gerry returned from Greece.

It wasn't just a question of that, though. She liked Steele's eyes, she liked his smile, she liked that she felt she could be honest with him. It would be such a relief to share what had been eating her up for these past couple of months.

'Have you ever slept with an ex?' Candy asked, quite sure, as she did so, that she was blushing from the roots of her hair to the tips of her toes.

'Doesn't everyone sleep with their exes?' Steele checked. He was so at ease with it all that she let out a breath that she felt as though she'd been holding in since it had happened.

'Well, I've only had two exes, and I only made that mistake with one of them.'

'Actually,' Steele added, 'I've never slept with my ex-wife. I knew from the day we broke up that we were done.'

He saw her swallow. And swallow Candy did—she had certainly thought him worldlier than her and that he had been married and divorced confirmed it.

'You sound bitter,' she said, and was somewhat surprised when he didn't deny that he was.

'I am a bit when I think about it, which I don't often do.' He smiled. 'She rang a few weeks ago and asked if we might consider getting back together. I long ago decided that I would never settle down with anyone again.'

He didn't reveal the initial reason for their break-up. There was no point. There was no need for in-depth explanations about his infertility, given that he wasn't going to be hanging around in any one place or in anyone's space for too long.

Though perhaps he needed to make that a little clearer to Candy, he realised. She was seriously gorgeous. The attraction had been instant for both of them, of that there was no doubt, but she was several years younger than him and a lot less jaded and he did not want to cause hurt.

'So you slept with your ex?' Steele checked, and she gave a glum nod.

'Do you know Gerry?' Candy asked. 'One of the head nurses in the emergency department.'

'I've never met him,' Steele said. 'But I heard a bit about him when I was looking into the waiting times in Emergency. He's an arrogant jerk apparently.'

'That's Gerry!' Candy rolled her eyes. 'He didn't used to be. He got beaten up by two patients a few months ago and it seems to have changed him.'

'He's the one currently in Greece?' Steele checked. 'The one who wrote "Glad you're not here" on his postcard?'

'That's the one.' Candy nodded. 'When I first moved out of home last year we went out, though not for very long.'

'You only moved out last year?'

'Believe me, twenty-four years of age is way too early in my family, unless it's to get married. I should only have moved out to marry the boyfriend they had sort of pressed onto me… Instead, I dumped him and rented a flat.'

'That would have been tough,' Steele commented.

'Yes, it caused a lot of arguments with my parents and I mean a *lot*, but in the end it was far easier to do that than marry someone just because my parents considered him suitable. Anyway, Gerry helped me a bit with the move, given that my parents were sulking. We went out for a while, like I said, but pretty quickly I ended it. That was last year but he's been having a few problems of late. He asked if we could go out for a drink a couple of months ago…' Candy gave an uncomfortable shrug.

'One thing led to another?' Steele checked, and she nodded.

'It was a complete mistake on my part—he thought that signalled we were back together and he wasn't best pleased to find out we're not. Since then he's been making things difficult for me at work. No one knows that we slept together again, thank God.' She looked at Steele, surprised she could meet his eyes after her big revelation. 'It should serve as a reminder—never get involved with anyone from work.'

'Too late,' Steele said. 'I think we both know we're heading for bed—guilt free.'

He liked it that she blushed and he liked it even more that she didn't disagree with him. Now was the time to make it clear that, though this could be incredibly pleasant, there was no question of it lasting for very long.

'I can assure you that I won't turn into a monster when we're over,' Steele said, not very gently spelling it out for her. 'I have very many exes who will tell you the same.'

Candy sat there as a delectable plate of roast beef, with all the trimmings, was placed in front of her. She was glad of the chance to think over his words rather than react immediately to them as she smiled and thanked the waitress. Steele was sitting there basically telling her that he was a playboy and warning her that before they started they had a use-by date hanging over them.

The strange thing for Candy was that she didn't mind. His openness was, in fact, refreshing. She was tired of games, tired of pretending she was enjoying herself. Tired of simply going along for the sake of going along. Gerry had got way too serious too soon, and Franco had been happy to marry her before they'd had so much as a coffee. She had been brought up with the expectation that any man she dated was a potential husband and had to somehow be a suitable provider. It drove Candy insane. She wanted to be twenty-four, she wanted to have fun, and with Steele she could. With him it was different—there were no games, just pleasure to be had with no expectation or end aim. There was something so unique about him, something that said she *deserved* to have sex with him at least once in her lifetime.

'What are you smiling at?'

'My thoughts,' Candy said. 'And they're not for sharing.'

'Would your parents be disappointed in you if they knew what they were?'

'Very.' She smiled.

'Good.'

'So you're here for six weeks?' Candy checked.

'Five now,' Steele said, 'and the last two of them without you, given that you'll be off on your holiday.'

Getting over you, she thought.

But, oh, at least she'd get to be under him.

That was the only sex Candy knew.

'Then where will you be living?' she asked.

'Kent,' Steele said. 'It's an amazing opportunity. I'm overseeing a complete overhaul of their geriatric department. I'm implementing an acute geriatric unit, where all medical patients will be admitted first.'

He had such energy for his job. Candy could hear it in every word he spoke. They had the loveliest lunch, chatting about work, about them, oh, about lots of things, but then Steele said he had to get back.

'I'm speaking with Macey's nieces at two. I'll give you a lift home...'

'I don't need a lift,' Candy said. 'I'm only two stops away.'

'You're sure?'

'Very.'

'So how will I know where you live when I come over to take you out tonight?'

'Where are you taking me?' Candy smiled.

'I haven't decided.' Out on the street he took her wrist and turned her to face him. 'Where would you like to go?'

Bed, she wanted to answer, when she had never felt or given that answer before. 'I'll leave it up to you. Though I warn you, I'm pretty wrecked. Night duty hasn't left me at my most sparkling.' She told him her address and he tapped it into his phone. 'I'll see you tonight about seven?'

'Sounds good.'

It was the middle of the day, there were people everywhere and yet when he took her in his arms it could have been the end of the most romantic night.

'Thanks for coming to lunch.'

'Thanks for asking me.'

It was a very new thing to her, to be somewhere simply because she wanted to be. It should be wrong, except it felt completely right. He was older, wiser and sexier than she had ever dealt with and she was more turned on than she had ever been in her life, and he hadn't even kissed her.

That was about to be corrected, though. Her heart was galloping even more than it had the first day they'd met. Right now it was almost leaping out of her throat in anticipation. An anticipation she had never known because when their lips met it seemed to set off a chain reaction. *This is what a mouth should feel like*, Candy thought, and *This is what a tongue was surely designed for*, she decided as his stroked hers.

Yes, there was a building anticipation because when first his body melded with hers Candy couldn't help but wonder what it would feel like if his hand moved a little higher, or how it would be if she moved in a little closer. Each question was answered—the sound of the traffic dimmed as their kiss intensified. She had never been kissed expertly before and his hand moved just a little higher than her waist to the edge of her rib cage and she ached for it to move higher still. His mouth, the pressure of his lips, the constant beckon of his tongue made her move in closer and she felt breathless.

Both rested their foreheads on the other's for a moment. Trust time to make things complicated, because if it had been nearly two a.m. they would be racing home right about now.

It was daylight, people were talking, a lazy Sunday afternoon was going on all around as they pulled back and met each other's eyes.

'Tonight' was the unspoken word between them.

Candy had never really looked forward to the night in that way before.

'I'm going to be late for my meeting,' Steele said as she got back to his mouth.

'You can be two minutes late,' she said.

She just needed one more taste.

CHAPTER FIVE

THANK GOD THAT she'd just had her period.

It had used to be Candy's excuse not to have sex, but as she had a lovely long bath and shaved and plucked and buffed her body into suitable Steele shape, she was grateful for that fact.

Yes, her Catholic guilt was hovering there in the background but she told it to please be quiet as she took her Pill.

She still hid them in her handbag. It was a matter of habit and her mother would freak, just completely freak, if she knew that Candy was on it. She'd come off it last year but, given what had happened with Gerry, she had gone back on it. She and Gerry had used condoms but what had happened had been such a surprise that she did not want to take any risks.

She hadn't gone home after lunch with Steele; instead, she'd dashed to the shops and bought fabulous underwear that she was now tearing the labels off. There was a silver-grey bra that gave her the best cleavage ever and silver panties that made her dimply bottom look fantastic. In fact, she was so impressed with them that Candy had bought a set in purple also.

She'd always felt fat, but she felt curvy now.

I'll regret it later, she promised her conscience as she looked in the mirror.

Just not yet!

With no idea where they were going Candy decided on a pale shift dress that would look casual with ballet pumps or fab with heels.

It didn't work with her new bra, though.

Second go.

A grey wraparound dress worked better, though showed a little more cleavage than her parents would consider suitable.

Perfect!

Not big on make-up, Candy put on some mascara and a slick of lipstick and when there was a knock at the door she was nervous, but nicely so.

'You're no help,' Candy said as she let him in and he handed her a bottle of wine. Steele was wearing black jeans and a black shirt. He looked incredibly handsome and had that air about him that meant he was suitably dressed for any venue.

'Meaning?' Steele asked.

'I was trying to decide whether to wear flats or heels given that I don't know where we're going.'

'We're going to the movies,' Steele said. 'I figured it might be nice if you're tired—though we shan't be making out in the back row. I like watching a film properly.'

'What are we going to see?' she asked. The movies was possibly the nicest place he could take her if they *had* to go out. It would be nice to turn her brain off for a couple of hours.

'Two choices,' he said. 'One is very dark, apparently funny in part. One is very sad… See what mood you're in.'

'I don't mind,' she said as she led him through her lounge and put the wine down on the bench of a very small kitchen.

'So this is what all the arguments with your parents were about?' Steele said, looking around the living room of her small but cosy flat. The front door opened to the living room. Off that was a small kitchen and to the side a hall that led to the bathroom and bedroom. 'It's nice.'

'I love it,' Candy said. 'It's a ten-minute walk to the Underground, a five-minute walk to my favourite Indian restaurant.

'We can eat before or after…' Steele said.

The thought of Indian before sounded too good to pass up, but then other senses were calling, the attraction wafting between them as potent as any delicious aroma from food.

Candy knew she was eons behind him sexually. She wanted to have slept with him, in part to have jumped that hurdle without knocking it over, in part just to dive onto the track…

And Candy usually hated even the thought of sport, but, oh, he was handsome.

And he was here.

'Do you want a glass of wine?' she offered, even though he'd brought it, but Steele shook his head.

'Not for me,' he said. 'I'm driving. You have one, though…' He went to open the bottle he'd brought but she stopped him.

'Not for me.' Candy shook her head. 'I don't really

drink and anyway I'm on early tomorrow. I'll just get my shoes.'

She went to her bedroom and put on flats but as she came out Steele frowned.

'What happened to the heels?'

'For the movies?'

'For me.'

She smiled and went and put on said heels, with Steele watching her from the doorway.

He made her shiver. If Gerry had stood watching her she'd have found it invasive, but with Steele she just wanted to strip off her dress, pull back the covers on the bed and climb in.

She could feel his eyes on her calf muscles and then on her bum and she turned and it was nice to feel provocative. It was something she had never felt before. He made her feel like this.

And he made her want to kiss him.

It was as simple as that, as natural as breathing to stand in the doorway of her bedroom and wrap her hands behind his neck and share a kiss for no other reason than they both wanted to. She didn't feel naïve or inexperienced with him. There wasn't enough space in her mind for those sorts of thoughts because it was filled instead with pleasurable ones as they got back to where they'd been on the street in record time.

Steele's hand did move higher than the base of her rib cage this time. He was stroking the underside of her breast as they kissed, and her nipples hardened and ached for his fingers to attend to them. She had one hand at the back of his head, just to feel his silky hair, not for pressure for there was plenty of that from Steele, and she had the other on his bum. His buttocks were taut and she checked again. Yes, they were still taut and it was that hand that demanded he press into her.

His moan to her mouth as he did so, his hand at the tie of her dress, told Candy there was no way they would be making the movie.

It was evening, not even semi-dark, and that was seriously uncharted territory for her. End-of-evening sex was all she was used to.

But this wasn't, oh, okay, then, it had been a week after all. This was, let me get this shirt open and this zipper down because I need you to take me now.

Her dress was open, his shirt too, and his fingers were at the back of her bra, ready to undo it, and Candy could barely breathe at the thought of their naked chests pressed together and his hot hands roaming her. She'd never had sex standing, never considered it, because she wasn't the tall, leggy version that a good Candy should be. She was a shorter, chunkier one, who any second now was going to scale Steele's body with the grace of a feline. It was that essential, that natural, that...

'Ignore it...' Steele said as there was a loud rap on the door.

'No...' She could barely breathe now but for a different reason. It was her father's very loud knock and she froze for a second.

'It's my parents.'

'Just ignore it,' he said again.

'They'll let themselves in.'

That her parents had a key came a close second to a bucket of water—actually, it beat the bucket of water because Steele was dressing her and himself with his hands as Candy stood there.

Then he chose to concentrate solely on her for now.

He did up her dress, a little loosely, and wiped off some lipstick and wished the flush on her cheeks would fade by the time she got to the front door. She looked as if she'd just come, or had just been about to. Her nipples were like the dials on his washing machine. Even her lips were swollen.

'Breathe,' Steele said.

'If they find you here...' Candy shivered as he knelt down and changed her heels to flats as there was another knock on the door.

'Will they have us married?'

'You have no idea.'

'Where do you want me?' Steele smiled.

'On my bed.'

'That's what I like to hear,' Steele said, then stopped joking. 'Are they likely to come in here?'

'I hope not.' Candy let out a breath. 'Probably not.'

'Relax,' he said as she closed the bedroom door on him and went to greet her parents. He checked under her bed and he could possibly fit there but first he smiled as he saw the scissors and labels from her brand-new underwear.

She was seriously gorgeous, Steele thought as he did up his shirt and wiped lipstick off. He was unused to thinking *seriously* anything about his dates yet she was so lovely, so focused on fighting for her independence and living her life and yet so kind.

Actually, right now, as Candy opened the front door all she was was stressed!

There were her parents buckling under the weight of jars filled with home-made tomato sauce.

'I said I'd pick them up next week,' she said.

'Why are you all dressed up?' her mother asked, instantly accusing.

'Because I'm just about to go out,'

'You need to wear a top under that dress!' Her mother warned.

They walked through and put the jars of tomato sauce on the bench and Candy got out the coffee machine. There was no such thing as her parents coming over and them not having a coffee, though her father's eyes lit up like a Christmas tree when he saw the bottle of wine on the bench and Candy poured him a glass.

'Where are you going tonight?' her father asked.

'To the movies with a friend.'

'What friend?' her mother checked.

'Kelly.' Candy glanced at the clock. 'Ma, I really do need to get going soon.'

'We've barely seen you these last few weeks.'

They chatted in Italian for twenty minutes or so. Candy had promised herself that the next time she saw them she'd tell them about her trip to Hawaii, but with Steele hiding in the bedroom she chose not to. It was not a conversation that would take twenty minutes— it would be an entire evening of tears and threats and shouting.

Her dad's wineglass was empty, her mum's coffee was gone and though they looked settled in for the evening and her father would no doubt love another glass of wine, Candy stood. 'I'm already late for Kelly,' she said. 'I really am going to have to get ready.'

She felt guilty kicking them out, and then cross that she'd had to. Couldn't they simply ring before they dropped around?

They'd be offended if she asked them to.

Talk about kill the mood, she thought once they had gone and she headed to her bedroom. Steele was lying on her bed, his legs crossed and reading her book.

'I'm so sorry about that,' she said.

'Why?' Steele shrugged. 'Your parents dropped around. It's no big deal.' He smiled at her as she came and sat on the bed beside him. 'I understand, though, that it would be a big deal if they found me here.'

'Thanks.' Candy smiled.

'Do they drop around a lot?'

'They do,' she said. 'They don't drive and, as a sweetener, when I moved out I said I was only moving nearby, which was a big mistake.' She let out a long sigh. 'Another one. I seem to be making rather a lot of them lately. Have I made us late for the movies?'

'I haven't even got the tickets,' he said. 'I didn't know if you'd like the idea.'

'I do,' Candy said, 'I haven't been in ages.'

'I go all the time,' he said. 'Well, not all the time, but I guess going to the movies, for me, is like reading a book is to you. I usually go on my own,' Steele said. It had surprised him that he'd considered taking Candy along. He really did prefer his own company when watching a film.

'How come you go alone?' she asked, gently poking him in the ribs as he lay there. 'Don't you have any friends?'

'I have a lot of friends but not any I'd want to go to the movies with. You should try going by yourself,' he said. 'I loathe trying to concentrate while getting the *What the hell did you bring me to this for?* vibe coming from my right or left.'

Candy started to laugh. 'I get that with my friend

Kelly.' She told him about the time she'd suggested to Kelly that they see what Candy had thought was a romance and he laughed as she described Kelly's reaction as she'd sat beside her, watching someone being tied to the bed.

'She said I was never allowed to choose the movie again,' Candy said, and then she looked down and saw that her hands were now on his chest and fiddling with his buttons and that his hands were playing with her hair. It was as if their bodies were having a little conversation of their own as they carried on talking.

His hand pressed the back of her head a little and she started to kiss him. Her heart was still hammering a bit from her parents' unexpected visit, and a long, slow kiss did nothing to calm it down, but slowly the turmoil of the sudden invasion by her family was fading.

His shirt was open again and beneath her hands were lovely flat nipples that she could not stop stroking, and her dress was open again and how she wished she had a front-opening bra, because she did not want to move her hands from his skin to get naked.

Steele peeled off her dress as she sat over him.

Till this point, till this evening, she had always felt that brief moment of judgment as she undressed. She felt only adoration now; she didn't even try to define what was going on in her head as her dress slid off. She did not care what he thought, safe in the knowledge he thought only good things.

He did think only good things. More used to slenderness, he adored her generous curves and her ripe breasts spilling as he undid her bra, but more giddying and satisfying was the mutual eagerness, as if they had somehow known this was where they were leading.

'I've got something I ought to tell you...' Steele said, pulling back.

'What?' she breathed. 'What do you have to tell me?'

He smiled at the dart of concern in her eyes.

'I'm not sleeping with you till I hear about your name.' His hand stroked one generous breast. 'Tell me,' Steele said.

'No.'

He pulled her onto him and then flipped her onto her back and she lay looking up at him, aching for his kiss. She had already kicked off her ballet pumps. All she had on were her panties and it was he who looked down at her now.

'I'm never going to tell you,' Candy said.

He stood and picked up his shirt.

'Come on,' he said. 'Get dressed.

'That's bribery.'

'Yep.'

Well, two could play at that game. 'Fine,' she said, half-heartedly sitting up, putting her legs over the bed and reaching for her clothes. 'Let's go and get something to eat...'

She picked up her bra and Steele took it from her hands.

He placed it beneath her breasts and did it up at the back and while he did so she could feel his breath on her shoulder and she was more than a little aware of his erection through his trousers. He took one of her breasts and gently stuffed it into the fabric but his hand stayed in there, stroking her, teasing her, and she sat still as his lips started to nuzzle the other one, licking and sucking at her nipple, stretching it with his lips as her hands moved to his head and urged him for more contact. But then he stopped. She looked down as he went to tuck her wet, very aroused breast back into her bra, and she decided he was cruel, so cruel that she knew if she didn't relent they would be sitting eating a curry or watching a movie about half an hour from now.

'Okay.' Her voice was all husky and she didn't really recognise it as hers. She cleared her throat, but it still sounded the same.

'As you know, my parents are Italian,' Candy said, and her head was on his shoulder as he unhooked her bra again.

'Okay.'

'Strict,' she said. His hands were now on her hips and she lifted her bottom to allow for him to take her panties down.

'Go on,' Steele said, which was contrary to his words because he was kneeling with his mouth on hers as she spoke.

'And they chose the most beautiful name that means pure and innocent...' she said, and she felt the stretch of his lips on hers as he smiled as she told him what she had sworn she wouldn't. 'And then when I hit my teenage years I noticed that people started to snicker and...'

'What is it?' Steele asked.

'What's the medical term for thrush?'

He pulled back and smiled. 'Candida.'

'Which is why I became Candy. Sadly, not to my parents. They still insist on calling me by my full name.'

'Were you teased?' he said to her mouth as his hand parted her thighs and his fingers slipped inside her.

Mercilessly.

'Poor baby…' Steele said.

'Oh…' Candy moaned, her thighs quivering.

He felt her thighs clamp around his hand and her head rest on his shoulder and there was that blissful choice whether to feel her come now or dive in for the pleasure.

Greed won.

He removed his hand and she let out a small sob of frustration combined with bliss as he stood and she sat naked, a breath away from him as he slid down his zipper and undressed. He handed her a condom and she shook her head.

'You do it.'

'You.'

Okay, she was bad at this part, except his erection was at her cheeks and she was licking her lips as she undid the foil. She had never seen something so lovely, so fierce, so tempting, and the quicker she did this and the quicker she came were very good incentives to get it on.

She played for a moment, loving the feel of him naked in her hands, teasing him with hot breaths to the head, cupping him in her hand.

'Candy.'

His voice was deeper, if at all possible, impatient and deliciously stern, and she would have loved to find out what might happen if she teased him further, dragged this out a little longer. Instead, she briefly looked up at chocolate-brown eyes that made her feel as sexy as hell.

'Put it on,' he said.

She did as she was told, unravelling it along his

lovely thick length and deliberately taking her time, loving the sound of his sharp breathing and then the impatient way he pushed her hands away when the job was done.

He pushed her shoulder lightly and it was like dominoes falling, because she toppled back on the bed and he lifted her legs abruptly for daring to keep him waiting. She was compliant, wonderfully so. *Talk about boys to men*, Candy thought as he seared inside her and then she wrapped her legs around him. It was like comparing apples to oranges. He knew exactly what to do as he moved deep inside her. His erection was so strong and fierce that each thrust took her to a place she had never been before.

'I'm going to come,' she said almost in apology, watching, feeling, arching to the bliss of him searing inside.

'I think that's the point,' he said, trying to hold on, revelling in the tight grip of her muscles and the tension of her as she came. It was so deep, so heavy, so intense that Candy briefly wondered if she'd even had an orgasm before.

He kept making love to her through it. She wanted to catch her breath, but then she didn't, for she loved the feel of him taking her as she came. Then she lost her head a little, stopped thinking about anything other than a very small bedroom and a whole lot of pleasure. Steele was looking down at her and then he stilled and she sobbed in pleasure as he started thrusting faster and released into her. To not come again would have proved impossible, to feel his tension release, to see this beautiful man above her and feel him come deep inside shot her into orbit again, her hand pushing at his chest, at the delicious hurt of a sensitive orgasm.

No regrets, never, she swore as, still inside, he collapsed onto her and they breathed their way back to consciousness.

He lay there, inhaling the scent of her hair, feeling her legs loosen and lower to the floor, and he knew this was different. Never had he been more perfectly matched in the bedroom. Her inexperience counted more than she knew for she melded to him, moulded to him. It was all he could do not to gather her things and carry her home.

And then normal service returned to his brain and he kissed her instead of saying the thoughts in his mind.

They ate at her favourite takeaway. A Formica table and cheap plates yet they fell on their food like savages, rather aware that sustenance might be needed later in this night, and then they headed for the movies.

'Sad or dark?' Steele offered.

'Dark,' Candy said.

They went to the blackest, grimmest, yet funniest film. He did watch it intently, yet the only reason he couldn't concentrate fully wasn't the *What the hell did you bring me here for?* vibe.

It was the *I really have to touch you* vibe that was coming from him.

'Stop it,' Candy said as his hand moved up her warm thigh and his mouth went for her neck. 'Concentrate.'

Futile words.

They were like teenagers, and that had been a long time ago for Steele and never for Candy. Those years she'd been keeping Franco at arm's length, not dropping her popcorn on the floor and necking.

'I'm going to have to come and see this alone.'

'So am I.' She smiled and got back to kissing him.

This was heading for morning, Steele knew.

This was heading to tomorrow evening and tomorrow night and the next morning too.

He had this vision of her parents arriving on the doorstep as her legs were behind her ears.

'Come back to mine tonight,' he said between kisses.

'Yes, please,' she agreed.

They weren't ready to be apart any time soon.

CHAPTER SIX

'HOW ARE YOU, Miss Anderson?' Steele asked the following Monday morning as he did his rounds.

'Macey.'

'How are you feeling, Macey?'

'A bit better.'

'That's very nice to hear,' he said as he examined her.

'How was your weekend?' Macey asked him.

'It was very nice,' he said, and she gave a soft smile.

He and Candy had been with each other for a week now. It had been the most intense week of either of their lives. Every available moment they had was spent together. Perhaps, aware how limited their time was, they were determined to make every moment count and were completely into each other. They were both exhausted but in the nicest of ways—between work and sex and eating, and dancing and drives at night just so Candy could find out what it was like to do it in a car, they were sleep deprived and loving it.

'Is Candy on this morning?' Macey asked, oh, so casually.

Steele answered a beat too late. 'I'm not sure what nurses are working this morning.'

'Well, I hope that she is. I haven't seen her for a few days.'

'I think she works in Emergency as well,' Steele said. 'From memory.'

'Does that mean that I won't get to see her again?' Macey fretted, or rather pretended to fret.

Steele knew when he was being played and he didn't mind a bit; he liked it that Macey was starting to notice things that were going on around her. 'I think Candy might be on duty later in the week.'

'Oh, that's good to know.' Macey smiled.

He had, on admission and again last week, interviewed Macey extensively and she had revealed nothing more but Steele pushed on. He knew where they were heading.

'I saw your picture in the corridor,' he said. 'They're putting up pictures of the history of the hospital as a part of the renovations. Emergency is getting a makeover at the moment and so too is the entrance corridor.'

Macey said nothing at first. She didn't want to hear about the changes to the hospital she had loved. It had been such a huge part of her life. 'I don't like hearing about renovations,' she said finally. 'I like remembering it as it was.'

'Things change,' Steele said. 'Not all things, though. Anyway, I saw you in one of the photographs. It looked as if you were getting a medal or a badge in the gardens...'

Macey's eyes filled with tears as she remembered those days.

'Can you talk to me?'

She shook her head.

'I want to see if I can help.'

'Well, you can't.'

'Okay.' He knew not to push her. Macey was starting to come out of her emotional collapse a little. The medicines were starting to help and she was engaging with the nursing staff and the occupational therapist.

He knew there was more, though, and that night he told Candy as he cooked them a stir-fry.

'Macey's holding out on me.'

'Maybe not,' Candy said.

'Oh, I'm pretty certain that she is.'

'How do you know?'

'I just know.' He smiled. 'Can you pass me the oyster sauce?'

She jumped down and went to the cupboard and got it for him.

'I hate this kitchen,' Steele said. 'It's really badly thought out.'

'I hate kitchens, full stop,' she said. 'You like cooking?'

'Not really,' he said, 'but I like eating.'

'Did you…?' Candy stopped. She'd been about to ask if he'd done the cooking when he'd been married. It was, she guessed, a no-go area, so she swiftly changed what she had been about to say. 'So why did you buy it if you hate it so much?

'It's just a serviced apartment.' Steele answered her question while knowing what she'd been about to say. He was used to avoiding such subjects with women he dated but Candy, or rather his feelings for her, was unlike any he had known and he was starting to come to grips with answering the tricky questions for her. For now, though, he was glad she had changed what she'd

been about to say. 'All my stuff is in storage. Which is
why I have to work out things like the coffee machine.'

'Oh! I thought you just need glasses. Well, I guess
that accounts for the terrible pictures on the walls.'

'I was about to say all my stuff is in storage apart
from the pictures,' he said, and then grinned at her
pained expression. 'Joke.'

'Thank goodness.'

She opened the bottle as he stirred in the beef. The
smell was incredibly strong, and she headed to the sink
for a drink and took a few breaths, not wanting to show
how the smell had affected her.

Tiny spots were dancing in her eyes and she was
sure that if she said anything then Steele would simply
tell her, as her parents had, to cut down on the extra
shifts that she was working.

'Are you okay?' he asked.

'Fine,' she said as she ran a glass under the tap. 'I'm
just thirsty.'

'You're wrecked,' Steele said. He turned off the wok
and came over and turned her to face him. 'You need
an early night.'

She smiled up at him. 'Our early nights are possibly
the reason that I'm so tired.'

'I'm serious,' he said. He looked at her pale features
and felt a touch guilty that she had been burning the
candle at both ends. 'Why don't you go to bed?' he
suggested. 'To sleep—a decent sleep.'

'It's seven o'clock.'

'Go to bed,' Steele said, 'and I mean to sleep. You
need it.'

'I think I might.'

Because they could, because they were both tired,

for no other reason than they wanted to, when Steele had served up their meals they headed to the bedroom, stripped off, Steele closed the curtains and they ate dinner in bed while watching the news. Candy felt very spoiled and very lazy as he took their empty plates through to the kitchen.

'I don't think I've been to bed at this time since I was seven years old,' she said as Steele climbed back into bed. 'I used to beg to stay up then!'

'Do you want to watch a movie or just go to sleep?' he asked, and they shared a very nice kiss.

'I just want to sleep.' She sighed, wriggling down in the covers and getting comfortable with him.

'Then do.'

She lay on his chest, delighted with their early night, feeling the lovely crinkly hair on his stomach and wondering if she'd ever been happier. 'I love your stomach,' Candy said.

'If you want to sleep you'd better stop playing with it, then.'

She didn't.

She thought back to what she'd been about to ask in the kitchen. Whether Steele had done the cooking or if his wife had was irrelevant, she knew. There was other stuff she'd like to know, though. 'Can I ask you something?'

'You can,' he said, staring into the semi-dark and sort of knowing what was coming and wondering how he'd answer it.

'Why did your marriage break up?

'We just didn't work out,' Steele said. Then he went to add his spiel about they'd been too young, or they'd just grown apart, yet he and Candy had always been honest with each other. They were *so* honest with each other that it sometimes took his breath away. Which meant he didn't want to be evasive now, yet he had never told anyone the reason for the break-up. He'd never told anyone apart from his ex-wife that he was infertile.

And when he had told Annie, she hadn't taken the news well.

'I haven't really talked about it before,' Steele admitted.

'Were you a wife basher?' Candy whispered.

'No.' He laughed.

'Then it doesn't matter,' Candy said, and gave him a light kiss on the chest. 'You don't have to answer.'

He wanted to, though.

'Annie and I got married when I was twenty-three and she was twenty-six. We'd been going out for years,' Steele said. 'We bought the house, the dog, all good…'

Candy didn't like that.

It was funny but she felt the little stiffening of her body as he gave his past a name and an age but then she breathed out through her nostrils and lay there, waiting for him to continue. 'Then Annie decided, or rather we both decided, to start a family.'

'She decided or both?' Candy checked.

'I thought we should wait but Annie really wanted children so we went for it but nothing happened,' Steele said. 'And then nothing kept on happening. I went and had a test—they usually check for issues with the guy first as it's far less invasive—and so we found out, pretty much straight away, that the problem was me.

I'm infertile.' He waited for her to stiffen again, or some sign of tension, or what, he didn't know, but instead she looked up at him through the darkness. '*That's* why you broke up?'

'Pretty much. Annie was devastated. I mean, the news completely sent her into a spin.'

'You broke up just because of that?' Candy asked. She really didn't understand.

'It causes a big strain in a marriage. Then there was all her family and how they dealt with the news.' Steele let out a sigh. 'Can you imagine your family's reaction if you told them that your husband was infertile?'

Candy thought for a moment and she could and so she answered him honestly. 'One, I'm not very keen on getting married…'

'Come on.'

'Seriously, I'm not,' she said. 'Two, I wouldn't tell them—it's none of their business. I might tell them that *we* were having problems if they nagged enough.' She thought about it some more. 'Steele, I do everything I can not to discuss sex and such with them—I still hide my Pills in my handbag.'

'I guess.' He smiled. 'After all, you hid me in the bedroom.'

Candy nodded to his chest. 'So I certainly wouldn't be discussing my partner's sperm count with them.'

Steele gave a low laugh.

'You said that she'd been back in touch?' she ventured.

'Yep, her second marriage has broken up and she asked if I would consider giving us another go, though with one proviso—there have been a lot of advances in technology apparently…'

'What a cow!'

He smiled. 'My thoughts at the time—well, a little less politely put in my head. I just hung up on her.'

'You didn't consider it.'

'I don't love her any more,' he said. 'I haven't for a long time.'

He looked a little more closely into the timeline of his marriage and divorce, something he rarely did. 'When I found out that I probably couldn't be a father and Annie had wrapped her head around the news, she lined us up for this battery of tests and investigations. She started to talk about donor sperm and, to be completely honest...' Steele hesitated; it hurt to be honest at times. 'I think I knew then that we had more problems than my infertility.'

'Like?'

He had never really examined it. He'd just shoved that into the too-hard basket, but lying there, her fingers on his stomach and her breath on his chest, he felt able to go further. 'Well, I'd always planned on being the complete opposite to my parents with my children. I didn't want boarding school or that sort of thing. I wanted to be a real hands-on father. When we first started trying to have a baby, though I thought we were maybe jumping in rather too soon, I was also looking forward to it. I think we all assume, or at least I did, that I'd be a parent one day. When I got the results I suddenly lost all that. I told Annie and she sobbed and she cried and then she had to go to her family and wail with them. It went on for weeks, and do you know what, Candy?'

She heard the bitterness in his voice and now she could understand it. 'What?'

'I was feeling pretty awful at the time. Seriously awful. I wanted some time to get my head around it. I wanted to process the knowledge that I couldn't have children. In hindsight we'd had it really good till that point. We'd never had to deal with anything major. And when we did, I found out that I didn't like the way Annie dealt with the difficult things that life flings at us at times. She made it all about her, not even about us. It was all about Annie. I tried to understand where she was coming from, yet she never did that for me. I think I fell out of love. If I was ever properly in love in the first place...' he mused. 'So, yes, while I've always thought that it was infertility that broke us up, I don't think it's that neat.'

He loved it that she was still there. She hadn't even jolted when he'd told her. Maybe because they were temporary, Steele pondered. Maybe because she wasn't worried about his ability to make babies, but it was nice to have said it and to have got such a calm reaction.

'Was she blonde?' Candy asked, and it made him smile.

'No.'

'Tall and leggy?'

'Go to sleep.' He was really smiling now as he kissed the top of her head.

'Can I ask another thing?' she said sleepily.

'You can.'

'Why are we using condoms?'

'Because I always have.'

'So have I.' She gave him a little nudge and Steele lay there smiling at the potential reward for his little confession. 'Well, they do say that every cloud has a silver lining.'

Candy didn't answer.

She was fast asleep.

CHAPTER SEVEN

CANDY HAD NEVER slept better than she did when Steele was beside her. His breathing, his heartbeat, the way he held her through the night were like a delicious white noise that blocked out everything else other than them. They wrapped themselves around each other, then unwrapped themselves when they got too hot and then when they got too cold found the other again. It was a seamless dance that lasted a full ten hours and had them on a slow sultry simmer that, by morning, started to rise to boiling point.

Candy awoke slowly, face down on the pillow and with her arms over her head. Steele's arm lay over her waist. The scent in her nostrils was Steele and as she started to wake up she remembered what they had been talking about before she'd fallen asleep. She knew it wasn't something that he'd discussed with others and the privilege of him confiding in her gave her a warm feeling. She loved it that he'd told her. She loved lying in bed next to him and feeling him start to wake up. She loved every minute of her time with him.

She felt his hand roam her spine. Steele's slow, lazy explorations made her melt into the mattress. It was as if each vertebra, right down to the lowest, was an individual treasure worth examining. His hand moved up her back and then to the exposed flesh on her side. Her rib cage received a significantly slower perusal, and his fingers found the softness of her flattened breast. She wanted to lift herself up to let his hand in but he rolled heavily onto her. His mouth buried beneath her hair, reaching for her neck, and then kissed his way to her ear.

'You do talk in your sleep.' His lovely voice greeted her ear and was just as effective in turning her on as his hands.

'Don't believe a word I say.' Candy smiled as he whispered to her the rude things that she *hadn't* said.

'How are you feeling now?' he asked, because it had been a very long sleep after all.

'Better than I ever have,' she admitted. 'I never want to move.'

'Then don't.'

There was a thrill low in her belly and Candy, who had never, till Steele, had morning sex, was fast becoming a fan as, still face down on the pillow, she felt Steele's delicious weight come fully on top of her.

Temptation beckoned as she parted her legs just a little, closing her eyes as his fingers checked that she was ready, which of course she was. Clearly last night's conversation was still on his mind because there was no pause in proceedings to reach for a condom and put it on. Instead, she felt his naked warmth nudging her.

He entered her slowly and Candy let out a moan and so too did Steele, because to feel her wet warmth along his length was intimate, way more intimate than he had been in a very long time.

His mouth was at her ear. 'Cross your ankles,' he said.

Candy did so and she thought she might collapse with the pleasure as together they started to rock—she could feel every long generous inch of him, hear his ragged breathing. Her face was red and sweaty in the pillow, and Steele took her hand and placed it between her legs and got to work on her breasts.

Oh!

She'd feel guilty later, Candy decided, but he didn't seem to mind a bit that she touched herself. They were barely moving, just rocking, his mouth was at her ear, his fingers stretching her nipples, and then his fingers slid down and took over from hers.

'You're bad for my conscience,' she said.

'No conscience needed,' he said.

He could go for ever like this.

Usually.

Her buttocks were so soft and ripe and they started to lift and press into his groin, and the soft muffled moans of pleasure had Steele tip just as she did and it was bliss to feel him come unsheathed inside her.

'Oh…' Candy lay feeling his weight on her and never wanting him gone. Even the alarm clock that was going off seemed a mile away.

'Can you wake me up like that tomorrow?' she said.

'I can.'

He rolled off and they lay, Candy still on her stomach, facing each other, and sharing a smile.

'I'm going to try and swap so I can get this weekend off,' Steele said, because she flew out the following Friday. 'It's not long now till you go.'

She didn't want to go.

Well, she did, because she was probably going to spend the entire first week of her holiday in bed. With all these extra shifts and sex marathons she was looking forward to sleeping round the clock.

She just wished that her holiday was scheduled for after he'd gone.

Then she stared into his eyes and wondered who she was kidding because she knew that she was going to spend her entire holiday sobbing. Despite starting off with the best of intentions to keep things light, to simply enjoy, Candy knew she was in way over her head. Her feelings for this man were so intense, so instinctively right that she simply could not imagine how she was possibly going to begin to get over him.

'Steele…' She took a breath. She wasn't sure if what she was about to say would sound too pushy, but she'd never held back from the truth with him and she chose not to now. 'Why don't you come for a few days?'

'To Hawaii?'

'Yes.' Candy nodded.

'I don't want to intrude on your holiday…'

'It wouldn't be intruding. It would be nice if you came in the middle. You've got a long weekend coming up.'

'It would be nice,' Steele said. 'I'd be pretty wrecked, though.'

'Well, I'll have slept for a week by the time you get there,' Candy said. 'I'll have enough energy for both of us. Think about it,' she offered, and then she climbed out of bed and grimaced when she saw the time. 'I'm going to be late. I'll have a quick shower and then I need to stop by my flat.'

'I'll drive you in,' Steele said. To keep things well away from work Candy was still taking the Underground and he watched the little flash of worry flare in her eyes.

'We might be seen,' she said. 'Steele, you've no idea how gossip spreads at that place.'

'I'm sure I do.' He smiled. 'It doesn't bother me if we're seen, unless of course it's a problem for you.'

She thought about it for a moment. 'Actually, no.'

'I can have broken your heart and put you off seeing anyone for ages after I've gone.' Steele grinned, giving her an excuse to give to Gerry if he pushed her to go out with him when he returned from Greece. But then Steele met her eyes and his tone changed slightly and she, though late for work, stood there in the bedroom and felt her heartbeat quicken. 'You could even say you were still seeing me,' he said, and they just looked at each other.

'I guess he wouldn't know either way,' Candy said, though something told her this conversation had little to do with excuses to give to Gerry.

There were two, possibly three, conversations going on.

That Steele would be gone and that Candy could say what she liked about them if it made things easier for her with Gerry.

That he would be gone, Steele thought, and he was saying that possibly this might last longer.

That he would be gone, Candy thought, and she didn't want him to be.

'Get ready,' he said.

They stopped at her flat and Candy quickly changed into jeans, which was what she usually wore for arriving at work, and rubbed some serum into her hair as she chatted to Steele.

'We came back here for this?'

'I can't leave home without it,' Candy said, trying to tame her long wild curls. 'I should buy another bottle and leave it at yours.'

'Why don't you just pack some things now and put them in my car?' Steele said, and she hesitated because she'd been thinking exactly the same thing. 'It would save us dashing back and forth all the time.'

She packed a case and they loaded it into his car and drove to work. It was all so new, so exciting that neither could help smiling.

As they pulled into the staff car park, Louise, a midwife who had done a stint in Emergency last year, was walking past. She and Candy had got on well. Louise was blonde and gorgeous and rather pregnant and she waved to Candy and gave a little wink.

'We're public knowledge now.' Candy smiled as she waved back, because Louise was a terrible gossip, which was surprising, considering that she was married to Anton, an obstetrician whose middle name was discretion.

'I'm fine with that,' Steele said.

He had long ago stopped playing games and this felt nothing like a game with Candy.

'We'll keep it discreet on the ward, though,' Candy said, because she was working on the geriatric unit today till lunchtime.

'Yes,' Steele said. 'I just don't want to be dropping you at another entrance and things. Come back to mine after work. I've got a meeting at six, though,' he continued, 'so I won't be back till about eight.'

'I'll have bread waiting in the toaster for you,' Candy said as he peeled off a key, which he had never done before. She snapped it onto her key ring as if it was no big deal.

It was a big deal. Both knew it. It was way too soon, but in other ways it was not soon enough.

Neither knew where this had come from or fully what it was.

They were planning holidays, her suitcase was in his boot, his key was now in her bag and they were kissing in the front seat as if one of them had just stepped off a plane after a year's absence. When she pulled back from his kiss, she returned to her question from before she'd fallen asleep. Candy was curious about his ex-wife and that spoke volumes in itself.

'*Was* she tall and leggy?' Candy smiled, watching him cringe just a little as he shook his head.

'Gamine?' Candy ventured. 'Please say no.'

'Not gamine *exactly*...' Steele said, and she groaned.

'Careful, Steele,' she warned. 'You may live to regret your next choice of words.'

He just smiled as they got out of the car.

There was nothing about their time together to regret.

Just that it was running out.

CHAPTER EIGHT

'I'M GOING TO take off your dressing, Macey,' Candy said. 'Steele wants to have a look at it.'

'Are you working tomorrow?' Macey asked, because Candy only had a four-hour shift and finished at lunchtime.

'I am, but I'm working down in Emergency.'

Macey was improving. Her medications were starting to kick in and she was engaging with the staff and other patients. She was also taking her meals unaided but she was still far from the feisty woman who had arrived in Emergency.

Steele came in just as Candy had got the dressing off. It was clearing up but it was very sloughy and still a bit smelly and as she saw it, Candy blew out.

'I'm just going to get the phone,' she said, even though it wasn't ringing, but she felt a bit sick. 'I won't be long.'

'I was like that,' Macey said to Steele, 'when I was...' Macey quickly changed what she had been about to say mid-sentence. 'When I was nursing.'

'No, you weren't,' Steele said. 'You weren't some young pup who couldn't stomach a bit of pus.'

Macey looked at him.

He knew. She was sure of it.

Steele did know because he had seen the cape carefully held to hide Macey's stomach in the photo in the entrance hall. He'd also done a little delving and it would seem that Matron Macey Anderson had gone to Bournemouth to recover from polio, though she'd made no reference to it when Steele had asked her for her medical history.

Tell me, his eyes said as Macey's own eyes filled with tears. Steele sat on the bed and took her hand. 'Talk to me, Macey.'

'When I was *carrying*, I was like that.' She started to cry as a fifty-five-year-old secret was finally released and Steele let her cry. He passed her tissues from her locker, not saying a word as Macey wept.

As Candy came in to do the dressing he briefly looked up to her. 'I've got this, thanks,' he said.

Candy saw that Macey was upset and left them.

When Macey stopped crying, he didn't press her for more information; instead, he did the dressing on her leg and afterwards he sorted out the covers. 'Do you want a cup of tea?' he asked.

'I'd like a sherry.'

'I bet you would,' he said. 'I'll be back in a moment.'

He took away the trolley, leaving Macey alone for a little while to gather herself. He left the curtains closed around her.

Candy was having a glass of water at the desk and he asked her for the keys to the cupboard where the sherry and things were kept and poured Macey a glass.

'Is she okay?' Candy asked.

'She will be. I'm going back in to talk to her,' Steele said. 'Macey saw you get a bit dizzy and has got you down as pregnant. I told her you're not and that they don't build nurses as strong these days.' He gave her a grim smile and then explained what was happening. 'As it turns out, she had a baby.'

'Oh…'

'Macey has never told anyone until now so it's a huge deal to her. I'm just giving her a few moments to gather herself,' Steele said, 'and then I'm going to go in and speak with her. Would you tell Gloria to make sure that we're not disturbed?'

'Sure.'

'If she has any visitors…'

'I'll say that the doctor's in with her.'

'Thanks.'

He walked back behind the curtains. Macey had stopped crying and she gave Steele a watery smile.

'Sorry about that,' she said.

'Why should you be sorry?' Steele asked, handing her the glass of sherry. 'I'm glad that you told me. Would you like to talk about it?' he offered.

'I don't know how to,' Macey admitted. 'It's been a secret for so long.'

'Not any more,' Steele said. 'It might help to talk about it.'

'I got pregnant when I was twenty-seven,' Macey said. 'He was married. I was never much of a looker and I suppose I was flattered. Anyway, my parents would have been horrified. They would have said that I was old enough to know better. We're never old enough to know better when it comes to matters of the heart, though. Instead of telling them, I confided in one of the matrons here. I thought she'd be shocked but she was more than used to it and took care of things. I was sent down to Bournemouth to have him. Everyone thought that I had polio and that was the reason I was away so long. Instead, I had my son and he was handed over for adoption.'

'I'm sorry, Macey,' Steele said. 'That must have been so painful.'

'It still is.' She nodded. 'I was very sick when he was delivered. I did everything I could not to push because I knew that as soon as he was born he would be taken away. I passed out when he was delivered and I never got to hold him and I never even got to see him. When I came around the next day I asked if I could have just one cuddle but I was told it was better that way. It wasn't.'

'Have you ever tried to look him up or make contact?'

'Never,' she said. 'I've thought about it many times but I didn't want to mess up his life if he didn't know he was adopted. I was told that he had gone to a very good family and that I was to get on with my life. I came back to work and threw myself into my career, but I've thought about him every single day since.'

'And his father?'

'I had nothing to do with him after that,' Macey said. 'We worked alongside each other for a few years afterwards. I think at first he thought he could carry on with me as before but I soon put him right. I told him to concentrate on his marriage. I'm very ashamed that I had an affair with a married man.'

'Try not to be ashamed,' Steele suggested. 'Perhaps it would be better to view that time with remorse but do your best to leave the shame out of it.

'I know you must have felt very alone at the time

but I can tell you from all my years doing this job that what happened to you happened to a lot of women from your generation.'

'He was married, though.'

'You weren't the first and you certainly won't be the last person to have an affair with a married man. My guess is you've more than paid the price.'

'I have.'

'Forgive yourself, then,' Steele said. 'Have you thought about discussing what happened with your nieces?'

'Sometimes,' Macey said. 'I wake up some nights, imagining them finding out what happened after I'm gone and not being able to speak about it with me.'

'Maybe consider speaking with them again,' Steele suggested. 'And if you want help telling them, or if you want me to do it for you, let me know.' He watched as Macey frowned, though it wasn't a dismissive frown. He could see that she was thinking about it. 'And if you never want to discuss it again, then that's fine too.'

'I might think again about telling them…' she said. 'There's just so much guilt. Sometimes when I'm enjoying myself I feel that I don't deserve to.'

'Let the guilt go, Macey,' Steele said. 'You are allowed to be happy.'

Candy sat at the nurses' station, staring at Macey's curtains, but, though usually she'd be curious, right now she wasn't wondering what was going on behind closed curtains.

Steele's throwaway comment about Macey thinking that Candy was pregnant had immediately been disregarded but now a small nagging voice was starting to make itself known.

She felt *so* tired.

Seriously tired.

There were many reasons that could account for that but the usually energetic Candy could barely walk past a bed without wanting to climb into it.

And she *had* felt sick a couple of times.

Actually, she'd had a bout of stomach flu a few weeks ago. Or she'd assumed it was stomach flu.

But she'd had her period, though it had been light, but she was sure that was because she had gone back on the Pill.

God, was it that fabulous bra that had given her such cleavage?

Stop it, Candy told herself.

Except she couldn't stop it.

'How is she?' she asked, when Steele came out from behind Macey's curtains.

'She's having a cry so keep them closed.' He told her a little about it. 'She doesn't want her nieces to know at this stage but at least she seems to be thinking about telling them.' He frowned at Candy's distraction. 'Are you okay?'

'I'm fine,' she said.

She wasn't, though.

Macey's words had seriously unsettled her.

Candy did her best not to let them.

She headed for home and looked around her flat. She opened the fridge to sort out the milk and things but let out a moan when she saw that it had already been done.

Her parents had been around.

Candy looked at a letter on her kitchen bench and saw that it had been opened.

It was her bank statement.

And there were flashing lights on her answering machine that Candy knew would be messages from her parents—they were really the only people who called her on her landline.

Candy took a breath and called her mum. She sat for five minutes wondering why it had to be like this as her mum demanded to know where she'd been and what she'd been doing.

'I've been really busy with work,' she said, loathing that she had to lie and then deciding not to. 'I've been doing a lot of extra shifts,' she explained, and took a deep breath. 'I've booked a holiday. It was a last-minute thing.'

'Where?'

'Hawaii. I go next Friday for two weeks.' Candy closed her eyes and tried to answer in calm tones as the questions started.

'I'm going by myself,' Candy said. 'I just felt that I needed to get away.'

No, she couldn't afford it and as she was told that Candy thought of the first day she had met Steele, who had simply said, 'Good for you.'

'Mum,' Candy interrupted. 'I'm going on holiday, I want to go and I'm not going to argue about it with you.'

'You listen—'

'No,' she said. 'I love you very much, you know that I do, but I'm not going to run everything that I do by you.'

It hurt to have this discussion but she knew it was way overdue. She knew they loved and cared for her and that they expected to be involved in every facet of her life. It just wasn't the way Candy wanted to live any more.

'Ma, I'm not arguing,' she said. She took a breath, wanting to tell them to please ring in the future before dropping around. She wanted to ask for the return of her keys but baby steps, Candy decided, so she dealt with that morning's events. 'Mum, I don't want you opening my mail and I've told you over and over that I don't want you coming around and letting yourself in when I'm not here.'

She meant it. So much so that when her mother pointed out she was just trying to help and, anyway, she'd need someone to take care of the flat while she was in Hawaii, Candy snapped in frustration. 'It's not a stately home that needs taking care of. It's a one-bedroom flat!'

It didn't go well.

Candy knew her requests would be, as always, simply ignored so after she put down the phone she did what she didn't want to but felt she had to.

She made a trip to the hardware store, but not just for locks. She also bought a drill.

Then she had to go back to the hardware store a second time because after numerous attempts her shiny new drill wouldn't screw in a nail but a very nice guy explained what a drill bit was for!

She loathed that she'd done it.

She loathed more than that that she'd had to, but she had realised that despite the move she hadn't really left home. Her parents saw her flat as a bedroom with a slightly longer hall to walk down. Candy thought of Steele hiding in her room that night and knew that was the reason they stayed at his place.

No, Candy thought as she turned the new lock on her door and then headed for Steele's, it was her life.

It was a long day for Steele.

A very long day.

He stopped by Macey's bed at the end of his shift and she asked if he would speak with her niece when she visited tomorrow.

'Of course I will,' Steele said.

Then he had a meeting to sit through, which really had nothing to do with him, given that he'd be gone in a few weeks. Not that it stopped him putting his point across about the lengthy waits in Emergency. Oh, and a few other things too.

By nine he should be more than ready for home but for once Steele was tentative.

There was no bread waiting for him in the toaster.

Steele walked through his apartment and put Candy's case, which he had bought in from the car, down in the hallway. He knew she was here and he knew where she probably was.

He walked through to the bedroom and, sure enough, there was Candy, fast asleep in bed with the light still on. He looked at her black curls all splayed out on the pillow and he looked at the dark circles under her eyes and he stood there for a full two minutes, watching her sleep deeply.

Steele made his own toast and then had a shower and tried to watch a film. It was a film that he had been meaning to watch for ages but, unusually for him, he couldn't concentrate.

There was something else, far deeper, on his mind.

He turned off the television and lights and got into bed next to Candy, and she rolled into him.

'Sorry,' she said sleepily. 'I saw the bed and couldn't resist. When did you get back?'

'Just now,' he said, though it had been a good hour.

'I changed the lock on my front door.' Her voice was groggy with sleep.

'Good for you,' Steele said. 'Go back to sleep.'

She did.

He didn't.

Instead, he lay staring at the ceiling.

Yes, there was a lot on his mind.

Macey's words had now seriously rattled him too.

CHAPTER NINE

After

CANDY WOKE IN Steele's arms and listened to the sound of his breathing.

She wanted him to wake and roll over and make love to her. She wanted the pregnancy thought in her head to be obliterated by his kiss.

Then she didn't want his kiss because she felt sick.

Candy's mind flicked over the past few weeks.

Yes, she'd been sick last month, but it had been one of those bugs.

Surely?

She really felt sick now and she crept to the bathroom and tried to throw up as quietly as she could.

It was exhaustion, Candy told herself, brushing her teeth and then showering, but when she glanced in the mirror she could see the fear in her eyes.

Steele lay there listening to Candy flush the toilet to drown out her gags and he blew out a breath.

'Morning,' he said a few moments later, when he came in and she was already in the shower.

'Morning.' Candy smiled but she couldn't quite meet his eyes.

There was an elephant in the room that they both chose to ignore and they dashed around, getting dressed, finding keys, exclaiming they were running late when really they were actually doing quite well for time.

There was the first uncomfortable silence between them as Steele drove Candy and the massive elephant in the car to work.

There was no frantic kissing and they walked through the car park in silence, Candy making the decision to do a pregnancy test as soon as she got there, Steele wondering what the hell he should say.

If anything.

The sound of an ambulance siren had her look up and she saw Lydia standing in the forecourt, frantically gesturing for her to run. Clearly there was something big coming in.

'I've got to go,' she said.

'Go!' Steele said, and he watched her run through the car park and to the forecourt, where not one but three flashing-light ambulances were now pulling up. Kelly ran past him too and as Steele walked up the corridor the anaesthetists and trauma teams were running down it towards Emergency.

Candy, Steele thought, was in for one helluva morning.

She was.

She raced into the changing rooms and stripped off her jeans and T-shirt and got into scrubs as Kelly did the same.

'What is it?' Kelly asked.

'Multi-traumas.' Candy passed on the little Lydia had told her as she'd dashed past. 'Four of them.'

'Four are coming here?'

It was rare to get four all at once but apparently there were several more critically injured patients going to different emergency departments. A high-speed collision, involving several vehicles, meant there would be nothing to think about other than the patients any time soon.

It was on this morning that Candy fell back in love with Emergency.

Yes, it was busy and stressful but it was what she loved to do. Helping out with a little girl who had looked dire when she'd first arrived but who was now coughing as Rory, the anaesthetist, extubated her was an amazing feeling indeed.

'It's okay, Bethany,' Candy said as the girl opened her eyes and started to cry. 'I'm Candy. You're in hospital but you're going to be okay.'

Thank God! She looked up at Rory, who gave her a wide-eyed look back because it had been touch and go. Bethany had had a chest tube inserted as her lung had collapsed in the accident and her heart hadn't been beating when she'd arrived in the department.

To see her coughing and crying and alive, Candy knew why she'd fought so hard to do a job she loved.

Rory and the thoracic surgeon started talking about sedation and getting Bethany up to ICU, and it all happened seamlessly.

'Busy morning?' Patrick, the head nurse in ICU, smiled when Candy came up with her patient.

'Just a bit.'

'You look exhausted,' Patrick commented. 'So this is Bethany?' He looked down at the little girl, who was sedated but breathing on her own. He nudged Candy away for a moment. 'I'm going to put her in a side room. I thought about putting her next to Mum but I think it's going to scare her more for now.'

'How is her mum doing?' Candy asked, because she had been so busy working on Bethany that she didn't really know what was going on with the rest of her family.

'Won't know for a while,' Patrick said. 'They'll keep her in an induced coma for at least forty-eight hours. Is it settling down in Emergency now?'

'I don't know,' she admitted. 'I haven't looked up yet.'

'Go and grab a drink,' Patrick said.

He was nice like that and Candy headed round to the little staffroom and had a quick drink from the fridge, pinched a few biscuits and then headed back to the unit.

It was quiet. One elderly man was being wheeled in on a stretcher and Candy rolled her eyes at Kelly as she walked into Resus to start the massive tidy up.

It was going to be a big job.

'Let's get one bed completely stocked and done,' Kelly said, 'just in case something comes in, then we can deal with the rest.'

They got one area cleared and restocked and were just about to commence with the rest when Lydia came in.

'I've asked if everyone can come through to the staffroom.'

'Now?' Candy checked, because there was still an awful lot to do.

'Just make sure that one crash bed is fully stocked,' Lydia said, 'and then come straight through. I need to speak to everyone.'

* * *

Steele's morning flew by too.

He had a video meeting with some of his new colleagues in Kent and arranged to go there next Thursday as he wanted to see how the extension was coming along. He also had a house lined up with a real estate agent and wanted to take a second look.

Mr Worthington passed away just after eleven, his radio on, his family beside him. Steele spent a good hour with the family afterwards in his office at the end of the ward.

As they left, instead of heading back out, he sat and thought about Candy. He didn't know how he felt and he didn't know what to do.

He looked up when there was a knock at the door and he called for whoever it was to come in then remembered that he'd asked Gloria to send Macey's niece in once the Worthington family had gone home.

'Hello, Dr Steele.' Catherine smiled. 'Gloria said that you wanted to talk to me.'

'I do,' he said. 'Come in.'

'Aunt Macey has just gone for an occupational therapy assessment,' Catherine said. 'It's nice to see her walking again.' She took a seat and then looked at Steele. 'It's bad news, isn't it...?' she said, and her eyes filled up with tears.

'No, no.' Immediately Steele put her at ease. 'I haven't called you in to break bad news about your aunt's health.' He watched her let out a huge breath of relief. 'Her physical health anyway,' Steele amended. 'But as you know, Macey's been depressed.'

'She seems to be getting better, though,' Catherine said. 'The tablets seem to be starting to work.'

'They are,' Steele said. 'She's talking a bit more and engaging with the staff. The thing is,' he said, 'it isn't just medication that your aunt needs at the moment. She's asked that I speak with you. There's something that's upsetting her greatly and it's been pressing on her mind.'

'I don't know what you mean.'

'Your aunt has something she wishes to discuss with you, a secret that she has kept for many, many years, and it's one she doesn't want you to find out about after her death…' He told her that Macey had had a baby more than fifty years ago and that he'd been given up for adoption at birth, but Catherine kept shaking her head, unable to take in the news. 'We'd have known.'

'Very few people knew,' Steele said. 'That's what it was like in those days.'

'But my aunt's not like that…' Catherine said, and then caught herself. 'When I say that, I mean she's so incredibly strict—she's always saying that women should save themselves and…' She stopped talking and simply sat there as she took the news in. 'Poor Aunt Macey. How can we help?'

'I think speak with Linda and then perhaps you can both come in together. Talk it over with Macey, maybe ask if she wants to look for her son, or if she simply wants it left. Her fear is that you'll find out after her death, whenever that may be, and you might judge her.'

'Never.'

'I know it's a shock,' he said.

'It is.' Catherine smiled. 'My mother would have had a fit if she knew. Is that why she's been depressed?'

'I think it's a big part of it,' Steele said. 'Maybe

when she's got it off her chest and spoken with her family, things can really start to improve.'

He was about to head down to Emergency to check to see if his new admission had arrived, but before he left he quickly checked some lab results and then scrolled through his emails. Then he checked the intra-mail as they were hounding him to go and get another security shot for his lanyard. He saw an alert that the Emergency Department had been placed on bypass and let out a sigh of frustration, because he really didn't want his patient ending up in another hospital.

He clicked on the intramail and, for a man who dealt with death extremely regularly, for a man who usually knew what to do in any given situation, Steele simply didn't have a clue how to handle this.

We are greatly saddened to inform staff of the sudden death of Gerard (Gerry) O'Connor, a senior nurse in the Emergency Department.

Gerry passed away after sustaining a head injury in Greece. Currently the Emergency Department has been placed on bypass as his close colleagues process the news.

He blinked when his pager bleeped and saw that his patient had, in fact, arrived in Emergency.

Steele considered paging Donald, his registrar, to take it. He wanted some time to get his head around things.

Yet he wanted to see how Candy was.

Steele walked into the war zone of Emergency. Resus was in shambles, though some staff, called down from the wards, were trying to tidy it up.

There were just a few staff around and he was surprised when, after checking the board, he walked into the cubicle where his patient was, to see Candy checking Mr Elber's observations.

'I'm Steele,' he said to his patient.

'Dr Steele, if you want to be formal.' Candy smiled at the elderly man as she checked his blood pressure. She was trying to keep her voice light but Steele could hear the shaken notes to it.

'I thought the place was on bypass,' he said to her as she pulled off her stethoscope.

'Mr Elber arrived just before we closed.'

'Can I have a brief word?' he said, and he watched her eyes screw up at the sides a fraction but she nodded and followed him outside.

'I'm so sorry,' Steele said, but Candy shook her head.

'Please, don't.'

'Candy—'

'Please, don't. I can't talk about it. I think I'm going to go home,' she said. 'Lydia offered.' She thought about it for a moment. 'I think I just want to go home.'

'Come round tonight,' Steele said, 'or I'll come over to you.'

'I don't want you to,' Candy said. 'I don't want to sit and cry over my ex with you. It's too weird.'

'It's not,' he said, but he didn't push it. 'Call me if you change your mind.'

'Thanks.'

Candy headed off and spoke with Lydia and said that, yes, on second thoughts, she was going to go home.

The news had come completely out of the blue. All

the staff were stunned. Candy had headed straight back out to the department, not really knowing what to do, when she'd seen that Mr Elber was sitting on a trolley and had been pretty much left to himself.

Now the complete numb shock that had hit her after finding out that Gerry was dead was wearing off and she was very close to tears.

And very scared too.

She changed and as she headed out of the department she saw Louise walking in on her way to work.

'Candy.' Louise came straight over. 'I just heard about Gerry. It's such terrible news...'

Candy started to cry but as Louise wrapped her in a hug, feeling Louise's pregnant stomach nudging into her was just about the last straw.

'I know you had a bit of a thing going on last year,' Louise said. 'It must be so—'

'Louise,' Candy begged, 'it's not that that I'm crying about.' Well, it was, but she certainly wasn't about to tell Louise the entire truth either. 'I think that I might be pregnant and I don't know what to do...'

'Come on,' Louise said, and led her to the canteen. There were groups sitting and talking, some from Emergency and in tears, so it didn't look out of place that Candy was crying.

Louise went and got them both drinks and then came over.

'How late are you?' Louise asked, knowing full well that Candy was seeing Steele—she'd seen them in the car after all.

'I'm not late,' Candy said. 'But I've been feeling sick and I'm so tired...' She knew it didn't sound much to go on. The awful thing was that she *knew* that she was. 'I simply can't be pregnant,'

'It will be okay,' Louise said. As a midwife she was extremely used to a woman's shocked tears when they first came to the realisation that they were pregnant.

'I don't think it can be,' Candy sobbed, 'and I can't tell you why.'

Louise sat and thought for a moment. If Steele was only here for a few more weeks, which was what she'd heard, then it wasn't any wonder that Candy was upset.

'I don't know who to talk to,' Candy said, and then blew her nose and told herself to get it together.

'Can you talk to me?' Louise offered. 'Do you want to do a pregnancy test? I'll come with you.' When Candy said nothing Louise pushed on. 'Could you talk about it with Anton?' Louise asked. Anton was Louise's husband and one of the most sought-after obstetricians in London. 'I was just on my way to have lunch with him so I know that he's got time to see you.'

Candy nodded.

It was time to find out for sure.

Louise took out her phone and sent a text and a few moments later she got a response. 'He says to come to the antenatal clinic and he'll see you. I'll take you over there now.'

'People will wonder what I'm doing in the antenatal clinic.'

'People will think we're just two friends catching up for lunch,' Louise said. 'Don't be so paranoid.'

As they arrived at the clinic Candy felt a moment's reprieve as she looked around at the pregnant women all sitting waiting for their turn to be seen.

She was overreacting, she told herself.

This world didn't apply to her.

'You might as well come in,' Candy said to Louise as they arrived at a door that had a sign with Anton Rossi written on it. 'He'll only tell you what's happening anyway.'

'God, no.' Louise rolled her eyes. 'Unfortunately for me Anton's all ethical like that. If you tell him not to tell me, then wild horses wouldn't drag it from him! You don't have to worry about that.' Louise gave her a lovely smile. 'But if you do want to tell me then I'm dying to know!' She gave Candy a cuddle just before she went in. 'You'll be fine.'

Candy really hadn't had anything to do with Anton before this. She just knew him by reputation and had seen him occasionally when he'd come down to Emergency to review a patient there.

'I'm sorry to interrupt your lunch break,' she said. 'Thank you for seeing me so quickly.'

'Louise said that you were very upset.'

Candy nodded. 'I know that everything is confidential but the thing is, this is terribly delicate and—'

'First of all,' Anton interrupted, 'you are right— everything you tell me is completely confidential. I never gossip.'

'Thank you.'

'I'm not even taking notes. Do you want to tell me what's happening?'

'I think I might be pregnant,' Candy said. 'The thing is, my partner...' She didn't even know if Steele was that but she pushed on. 'It can't be his.'

'Because?'

'He's infertile.'

'Have you been seeing someone else?' Anton asked

gently—he was used to that being the case—but Candy shook her head.

'I've only been with my current partner for a couple of weeks. We weren't supposed to be serious, but…' It sounded so terrible put like that but Anton's eyes were sympathetic rather than judgmental. 'I had a one-night stand with my ex a couple of months ago.' She thought back. 'Three months, maybe. We used condoms.'

'Nothing is fail-safe,' Anton said.

'I went on the Pill afterwards,' Candy said. 'I wasn't expecting anything to happen again but I just decided I wasn't coming off it. I have had my period.'

'A normal period?' Anton checked.

'It's been light but I thought that was because the day I got it I started the Pill.'

'The first thing we need to do—' Anton was very calm '—is to find out if you are indeed pregnant.'

He gave her a jar and a few minutes later she sat in his office and she knew, she simply knew that she was. A few moments later Anton confirmed it.

'Candy, you are pregnant.'

He let it sink in for a moment.

'How do you think your partner will react?' Anton asked.

'I don't think I'm going to find out,' Candy said, and she just stared at the wall. 'There's really no point telling him. We both agreed from the start—'

'What about the father?'

Oh, that's right. Candy's brain was moving like gridlocked traffic. It was like telling a joke and forgetting the punch line, because she hadn't told Anton the good part yet. 'You know Gerry, the head of nursing in Emergency…'

'Oh, Candy.' Immediately he took her hand. Anton didn't gossip—in fact, he had been in this office all morning—but he had seen the email twenty minutes or so ago informing everyone that Gerry had passed away while on holiday in Greece and that Emergency was on bypass.

'I don't know what to do.'

'Of course you don't know what to do at the moment,' he said. 'This is all too much of a shock. How long have you been worried that you might be pregnant?'

'Since yesterday,' Candy said. 'A patient said something. I know I'm a bit overweight, it just…'

'Hit home?'

Candy nodded.

'I knew you were pregnant before I did the test,' Anton said, which concerned him a little as it did not seem to fit with her dates. 'We could do an ultrasound now, here, and see exactly where we are,' he suggested. 'Are you ready to do that?'

She nodded.

'Go to the examination table and undo your jeans. He came over and had a feel of her stomach but said nothing—though he was starting to think that Candy would soon be in for another shock.

He squeezed some gel on and turned the machine away from her. 'Can you turn the sound off, please?' Candy said, because she didn't want to hear its heartbeat.

'Of course I can.'

He took a few moments, running the probe over her stomach and pushing it in over and over.

'I really am sorry to interrupt your lunch break,'

Candy said, more for something to say because she was dreading the next conversation.

'My wife would have been nagging me to do an ultrasound on her anyway.' He smiled and then he looked across at Candy. 'I shan't be discussing this with her.'

'Thank you.'

He had finished.

'Stay there,' Anton said as she went to sit up. 'You are close to thirteen weeks pregnant, which means conception was eleven weeks ago.'

'I've had my period, though.'

'Breakthrough bleeding,' Anton said. 'Nothing to worry about. All looks well on the ultrasound. Obviously your hormones are everywhere right now.'

'Would the Pill have harmed it?'

'No. Many, many women I have seen have taken the Pill while not knowing that they are pregnant. You've had no symptoms?' Anton checked.

'Not really.' Candy shook her head and then lay and thought back over the past few weeks. 'I had what I thought was a bug and I've felt sick a couple of times and been a bit dizzy, but I never really gave it much thought.' She looked up at Anton. 'I've been so tired, though. I mean *seriously* tired. I actually booked a holiday because I was feeling so flat.'

'Candy,' Anton said gently, 'I'm not surprised that you have been feeling exhausted—it's a twin pregnancy.'

It was just as well that he had kept her lying down.

Candy lay there, stunned, trying and failing to see herself as a mother of twins. Finally she sat up and when she took a seat at the desk Anton gave her a drink of water.

'I don't know what to do.'

'As of now,' he said, 'I would expect that your mind is extremely scattered. Is there anybody that you can talk to about this?'

'Not really. My parents will freak,' Candy said, panicking just at the thought of telling them. 'I can't tell anyone at work or it will be everywhere.'

He nodded in understanding but he was practical too. 'You are going to start showing very soon—in fact, you are already,' Anton said. 'I could feel that you were pregnant before I did the ultrasound. Your uterus is out of the pelvis and you will show far more quickly with twins.'

'I can't have it, Anton,' Candy said, but then she started to cry because it wasn't an it. It was a *them*.

'Candy, you do need a little time to process this news but you also need to come and see me next week. You don't have much time to make a decision. I do want you to take the time to think very carefully about this.'

She didn't need the time. In that moment, she had already made her choice.

'I can't...' Candy said, and then took a deep breath. 'I'm not having an abortion.'

'Well, you have a difficult road coming up,' Anton said, 'but I can tell you this much—I will be there for you and in six months from now you will have your babies and today will be just a confusing memory.'

'Thank you.'

They chatted some more and Candy told him that she was booked to go to Hawaii next week. 'Can I still go?'

'Absolutely!' he said. 'It will be the best thing for you. Let your insurance company know. Put me down as your obstetrician. I do still want to see you next week, though. You need to have some blood tests and I want to go through things more thoroughly with you. Right now, it's time for the news to sink in.'

Poor thing, Anton thought as she left his office. He had looked after many women whose partner and even ex-partner had died and knew that it was a very confusing time.

He smiled as there was a knock at the door and Louise came in. 'How was she?'

'She's fine,' Anton said, and then rolled his eyes as Louise picked up the gel. 'Step away from the ultrasound machine, Louise.'

'Please,' Louise said. 'It's wide awake. I can feel it kicking.

'Because it probably knows its lunchtime,' Anton said. 'Come on, I would actually like to get some lunch.'

'Is Candy okay?' Louise shamelessly fished as they walked down to the canteen. Anton absolutely trusted his wife but part of what he adored about her was that she could not keep a secret and so, to be safe, he said nothing.

'She's on with him...' Louise nudged.

'Who?' Anton frowned.

'The sexy new geriatrician that just walked past,' Louise explained. 'Candy is on with him.'

He loathed gossip, he truly did, but, unusually for Anton, he turned his head.

He felt sorry for her new partner too and tried to imagine how he would feel if his gorgeous wife had already been pregnant when they'd met.

Anton was man enough to admit that he didn't know.

* * *

Candy stepped into her flat and put down her handbag and she didn't know where to start with her thoughts.

Just after seven there was a knock at the door and Candy opened it to the angry questions and accusations of her parents.

'Where were you?' her mother asked, and demanded to know where Candy had been last night and the night before that.

'We came over and you were not home.'

'Please, not now,' Candy said.

Yes, now.

'For the last two weeks you are hardly home. We call around and the lights are off. We telephone and you don't pick up.'

'I'm twenty-four years old, Mum,' Candy said. 'I don't have to account for my time...'

She might as well have thrown petrol on the fire because all the anger that had been held in by her parents since Candy had moved into her flat came out then.

She was heading for trouble, her mother warned.

They didn't raise her to stay out all night.

Who was she going to Hawaii with?

Candy thought of Steele then and stood there, remembering the beginning of tentative plans.

How much simpler life had seemed then.

'I'm not discussing this,' Candy said. 'I'm very tired. It's been an extremely long day.'

She simply refused to row.

When they finally left she stood in the hall.

No one understood. Her friends at work thought she was ridiculous to worry about what her parents might think, but she did. Candy loved them. She just didn't know how to be both herself and the daughter they demanded that she be.

Imagine telling them that the she was pregnant.

She simply could not imagine it.

Not just pregnant, but pregnant with twins and the father was dead.

Candy dealt with things then as any rational, capable adult would.

She undressed, climbed into bed and pulled the covers over her head.

CHAPTER TEN

'HI.'

Steele could hear the tension in her voice when Candy called him on Saturday, though she was trying to keep her voice light.

'Hi, Candy.'

'Is it okay if we give it a miss tonight?' she asked. They had planned to go to a stand-up comedy and the tickets had been hard to come by.

'Of course it is,' he said. 'I doubt you're in the mood for laughing out loud. Do you want me to come over?'

'I'd really just like a night on my own,' she said.

Another one.

And then another.

And then another.

On Tuesday, four days before she flew, Steele saw her briefly in the admin corridor. She was coming down from Admin, where she had been trying to sort out her salary for her annual leave when she bumped into him.

'How are you doing?' he asked.

'I'm fine,' she said. 'I actually can't stop and speak. Lydia has messed up my annual leave pay and I've been trying to sort it out.'

He walked in the direction of Emergency with her. 'How's the mood in Emergency?'

'Pretty flat,' Candy said. 'His funeral is being held in Sunderland, where he's from, but the hospital is holding a memorial service for him. They're naming the new resuscitation area after him,' She gave a tight smile. 'Thankfully I'll be in Hawaii when it's held.'

'Thankfully?'

She shook her head. She really didn't want to discuss how mixed up she was feeling right now, especially with Steele. She had considered changing her holiday so she could attend the memorial service but the thought of facing his parents there was too much for Candy. While she knew she had to tell them, she wanted to get her own head around it first. As for them naming Resuscitation after him! Well, the thought of wheeling patients in and out of Gerry's Wing, day in and day out, had her stomach in knots.

Then she turned and looked at the man she was quite sure she loved with all her heart and she wanted to break down and tell him. She wanted the pregnancy to go away and to be back to where they had once been, but it certainly wasn't Steele's problem so she gave him a very tight smile. 'I do have to go.'

He nodded and watched her dash off.

Leave it, the sensible part of his mind said as he headed back to the geriatric unit and went and hid in his office.

He was certain now that Candy was pregnant. In a matter of days her body had changed and she was completely unable to meet his eyes.

He was roused from his introspection by a tap at the door and he called for whoever it was to come in.

'Sorry to trouble you.'

'No trouble at all.' Steele smiled at Catherine, Macey's niece and another woman.

'This is my sister, Linda.'

'Good afternoon, Linda.' He expected Linda had some questions, that they perhaps wanted to know how best to broach things with Macey. But, as Steele found out every day in his job, there were always surprises to be had.

'When Aunt Macey had her heart attack,' Catherine started, 'Linda took care of her home, fed the cat, that sort of thing...'

'I see.'

Linda spoke then. 'A letter came while she was in hospital. I was doing her mail and paying her bills so she didn't have to worry about being cut off. I opened this letter and it was from a charity that deals with adopted children. It explained that Macey's son wanted to make contact. I didn't know if it would make things worse. She was so sick...'

'Of course you didn't know what to do,' he said.

'I didn't even tell Catherine,' Linda said. 'I just didn't know what to do with the news. I spoke to my husband and he suggested that we wait till Aunt Macey was feeling better. Really, though, she's been slowly going downhill for so long...'

'Do you have the letter with you?' Steele asked, and she nodded and handed it to him.

'He wants to make contact,' Linda said. 'I feel bad for not telling her.'

'Don't feel bad,' Steele said. 'It could have been an

awful shock for her, though now I think it will be very welcome news. Why don't you go in now and speak with her? Facing it will be hard and I'll be around if she gets upset but, to be honest, I think it will be a relief.'

He did hang around, but all seemed calm with Macey. He sat at the desk next to Elaine. He could see Macey and her nieces talking earnestly and at one point Macey actually laughed.

'It's good to see her laughing,' Steele said, and turned and smiled at Elaine.

'Sorry?'

'Macey,' Steele explained, then he saw Elaine's swollen eyes. 'Are you all right, Elaine?'

'I am.' She gave a small shake of her head. 'I'm worried about my assessment.'

Steele frowned. 'Elaine, you're doing really well. I know I'm not a nurse, but I do know how well you look after the patients.'

'Even if I get my words wrong at times,' Elaine said, because Abigail had had a small word with her about the muffy thing.

'Even if you get your words wrong.' He smiled, and was pleased to see that she did too. 'Is there anything else on your mind?'

'No.' She shook her head and stood up and left him sitting alone.

Steele looked over again at Macey and her nieces and knew it was time for him to take his own medicine.

It was time for him to face things.

When he arrived in Emergency he saw the smudges beneath Candy's eyes and she was still refusing to meet his gaze.

Direct as ever, Steele asked the question. 'Are you avoiding me?'

She stood there and went to lie to him, to say of course not, or whatever, but his beautiful eyes demanded the truth so she nodded. 'Yes.'

'Can I ask why?'

There was no point in telling him about the pregnancy so she made up an excuse. An excuse that was partly true. 'I've been a bit mixed up about Gerry and I had a big argument with my parents. They've realised that I've been staying out at night...'

'Really?' He looked at her for a long moment. He knew she was lying, knew how she'd fought for her independence and knew too that she wouldn't give in to them.

'I think we should just leave things,' Candy said. 'I don't want to upset them.'

'I don't believe you,' he said. 'While I understand you might need a bit of space after what's happened to Gerry, I don't believe that's it.' When Candy didn't respond he pressed on. 'Do you know, one thing that I've really enjoyed about our time together is how honest we have always been. It's fine if you want to end things, but at least tell me the reason why.'

'Can we go somewhere private?' she asked.

'Sure,' he said, his voice clipped. 'My office?'

They walked through the hospital in silence and then onto the geriatric unit and it felt to both of them as if they were walking to the gallows—which they were, for this killed them.

Through the ward they went and to his office at the end, and Macey watched their strained faces as they passed by.

Candy stepped into his office and didn't take a seat. She had a feeling she wouldn't be here for very long.

'Do you want to tell me what's going on?' he invited.

'Not really,' she said.

'Okay. *Are* you going to tell me what's going on?'

'I'm pregnant,' Candy said.

For Steele it was the strangest sensation. Ten years ago he had wondered how he might react when the woman he was crazy about told him such news.

Now, ten years on, the woman he was seriously crazy about was telling him such news.

'With twins,' she added.

He hadn't been aware that she'd brought a cricket bat with her when she'd come into the office. Of course Candy hadn't but it felt like that as she added her little postscript and he was left with one thought, one regretful, sad thought.

They're not mine.

'They're not yours,' she added, like an echo to his brain, and Steele snapped his response, in his gruff, low voice.

'I think I'd already established that, thank you.'

Yes, he actually felt as if he'd been knocked on the back of the head because his reactions, his words did not belong to the man he knew he was, yet, concussed by the impact of her news, he continued to speak. 'What do you want me to say here, Candy?'

'I don't know,' she admitted.

He honestly did not know how to react. Was he supposed to step in and say, *That's fine, darling, I'll raise his babies*? Or, *How convenient, Candy*, he should perhaps say with a smile, *given that I shoot blanks.* Or was he supposed to say that it was no big deal?

It was a massive deal.

He should, Steele knew on some level, take her in his arms and tell her that things would work out, that she could get through this.

His arms couldn't move, though, and his mouth was clamped closed so that no words could come out.

'I'm going to go,' she said.

'Wait.'

'Why?' Candy answered. 'Steele, we agreed to three weeks. We managed two. I was hoping to get through this week without telling you.'

'But you have.'

'Because you're right—we *have* always been honest. Yes, I've been avoiding you. I didn't want to spoil what we had.'

'Have you told your parents?'

Candy shook her head.

'Have you told anyone?'

'I have now,' she said, and she looked straight through his eyes and to his heart. 'I've got the hardest part out of the way now.'

And telling Steele *was* the hardest part. Her parents, Gerry's parents, all of that she would deal with in time, but this part hurt the most.

'I'm going to go,' she said again. 'If you could drop my case off that would be brilliant. Just leave it at the door.'

She walked out then and he sort of came to and opened his office door and stepped onto the ward. There was Candy, walking out quickly, and he closed his eyes in regret for his lack of response. Then he turned and saw that Macey was watching him.

No, Steele did not smile.

Instead, he walked up to the nurses' desk. 'I'm going home,' he said to Gloria. 'Page Donald if you need anything.'

CHAPTER ELEVEN

IT WAS A long lonely night for both of them.

Candy woke in her flat and was more tempted than she had ever been in her life to ring in sick this morning. She had a shift on the geriatric ward, her last one. She was desperate to avoid Steele yet she wanted somehow to see him. And to see Macey too and say goodbye.

Then she had two more shifts in Emergency and then she flew to Hawaii.

Alone.

Or rather not alone—she ran a hand over her stomach and felt the edge of her uterus.

She had no idea how she felt about being pregnant.

No idea how to tell her parents or friends or anyone.

Right now, none of it even seemed to matter.

She loved Steele.

It wasn't like the crushes she'd had on other men, which Candy was rather more used to.

It felt so much deeper than that, like an actual concrete thing that now resided within.

Except the twins resided within also.

Twins?

As he did up his shirt that morning Steele was thinking about them too.

He was also thinking about her words—how telling him had been the hardest part.

He knew how impossible her parents were and he knew telling Gerry's parents would be supremely difficult.

Yet telling him…

As he did up his tie, he found himself closer to tears than he had been at his marriage break-up. Closer to tears than he had been at his grandmother's funeral.

In fact, Steele wasn't even close to tears—he was sitting on the edge of the bath in a serviced apartment, bawling his eyes out, for the fact they were over and the grief that her babies were not his. He'd never cried. Even when he'd found out that he couldn't have children, Steele hadn't broken down. He'd been too busy mopping up Annie's tears. Now, ten years later, he let out what had long been held in. He cried alone.

He was as nice to himself as he had been to Macey.

At seven a.m. it was a bit early for sherry but he made a strong mug of tea and put in extra sugar and then sat and thought what best to do.

He could avoid Candy, Steele knew. He could call in sick today. He had a day off tomorrow and then it was just her final shift in Emergency on Friday—he could send Donald to deal with anything that came up in Emergency, and he would never have to see Candy again.

He couldn't do that, though.

'Morning,' he said as he came into the kitchen on the geriatric ward, and there was Candy, making a mug of tea.

'Morning,' she said, though she brushed past him pretty quickly and headed off for handover.

Steele headed into his office and checked his emails.

Oh, joy.

There was Gerry.

His smiling face was surrounded by flowers, and Steele, along with the entire hospital—as long as cover could be arranged, of course—was invited to attend the memorial service next Tuesday and the naming of the resuscitation area as Gerry's Wing.

Candy was trying to get her head around that terrible name too.

Lydia, who had been on the edge of taking disciplinary action against Gerry, was now talking about him as if he'd been an angel—an angel with one wing—a wing named after him that Candy would work in, walk through, deal with day in and day out...

As Candy helped Macey shower, she was wondering how the hell she could continue to work there. Kelly had given her an odd look in the changing room yesterday and a little huddle at the nurses' station had suddenly gone very quiet when she had approached.

No one had had the nerve to outright ask her. Candy was quite plump and they were clearly trying to work out if she'd been hitting the doughnuts or if indeed she was pregnant.

Imagine them knowing she was pregnant by Gerry.

'You're very quiet this morning,' Macey said as Candy turned off the taps and helped her to get dried and dressed.

'I'm sorry, Macey, I was miles away.'

'Dreaming of Hawaii, no doubt,' Macey said. 'Are you looking forward to your holiday?'

'I am,' Candy said. 'I fly on Friday night.'

'It's Wednesday today.' Macey smiled. 'I think for the first time in years I actually know what day it is.'

'You're so much better,' Candy commented, as Macey dressed herself with just a little help. When they got back to the bed, Candy would remove Macey's dressing for Steele to have a look at her leg ulcer, which was doing much better. After lunch, Macey would lie on the bed for a couple of hours' sleep, but apart from that she sat in the chair or walked to the day room. It was wonderful to see the improvement in her.

'Steele says I should be able to go home next week.'

'How do you feel about that?' Candy asked as she walked with Macey back to her bed.

'I'm looking forward to it very much,' Macey said. 'I'm having some modifications done to the bathroom and kitchen, which my niece Linda is sorting out for me. Things will be a lot easier now.'

'Your nieces seem very nice.'

'Oh, they're wonderful women.' Macey nodded, taking a seat by the bed and putting her leg up on a footstool. She watched as Candy made up the bed. 'You've earned your holiday,' Macey said. 'I wish I could be here to see the postcard.'

'I'll send you one, Macey.' Candy smiled, despite her earlier declaration about not sending any. 'If you're okay with that?'

'Oh, yes, please! It would make my day! Is it just you going?'

Candy nodded.

'Hawaii would be a beautiful place to go with the right man…'

'It would,' Candy agreed, her heart twisting as she thought how close she had come to sharing a part of her holiday with Steele.

'You don't have a boyfriend, though,' Macey continued. 'If I remember rightly.'

'No.'

'And you're carrying?' Macey said gently, and Candy's eyes filled with tears as she nodded.

'I'm having twins.'

'Congratulations, my dear.'

Macey was the first person to offer congratulations and she said it so nicely that Candy started to cry.

'Pull the curtains,' Macey said.

'No, no.' Candy sniffed. 'I'll go to the staffroom.'

'You'll pull the curtains and sit with me for a while.' Macey's orders were clear and Candy did as she was told.

'Have you told…?' Macey hesitated. She had been about to ask if Candy had told Steele, if that was what the argument the other day had been about, but her sharp mind was returning. Macey sat quietly for a moment, remembering when she had been admitted and had snapped at Steele for being a locum. It had only been his second day here, Macey recalled.

Certainly there had been a romance between Candy and Steele. She had seen it unfold in front of her own eyes.

'Have you told the baby's father?' she asked instead.

'Macey…'

She saw Candy swallow and reached out to take

the hands of the younger woman to encourage her to speak on.

'I made a mistake a few months ago, so please don't feel sad for me when I say this—I'm not a grieving widow. The baby's father died a week ago.'

'Gerry?' Macey said, and watched Candy's eyes widen in surprise. 'I hear all the gossip.'

'Yes.' Candy gave a watery smile. 'It was him.'

'That's very sad.'

'It is,' Candy said. 'I don't know how he'd have felt about it,' she went on. 'We wouldn't have got back together but I'm sure we'd have sorted something out.'

'What about Steele?' Macey asked, and she watched the tears spill down Candy's cheeks, though she neither confirmed nor denied there was anything going on.

'You have your holiday to look forward to,' she said, and Candy nodded. 'It's a good job you booked it before you knew.'

'Oh, yes,' Candy said, because it would be her first and last overseas adventure alone. 'I don't think I'll be lounging around on the beach next time I go. It will be buckets and spades...' She shook her head. 'I can't see how I'll manage,' she admitted.

'You know, I can remember being alone and pregnant,' Macey said. 'I expect it's still a very scary place even fifty years on, even with all the choices you girls have these days. I still remember how scared I felt when I got pregnant but I'll tell you this much—by the end of my pregnancy I wasn't scared about having a baby. I wanted him so much and I know you'll feel the same way about your two.'

Candy nodded. She knew Macey was right. 'I'm sorry for what happened to you, Macey.'

'I know you are but don't be sorry. My nieces are getting into contact with him. If I can see him just once I'll be happy…' Her voice trailed off and she looked up and Candy followed her gaze and saw that Steele had popped his head in.

'Sorry,' Candy said, standing up from the bed. She was supposed to have removed Macey's dressing and she was embarrassed at him seeing her cry.

'It's fine,' Steele said. 'I'll come back later.'

He left them to it. He was glad that Candy was having a chat and a cry with Macey and when she came out a little while later and told him Macey's dressing was down, instead of ignoring what he'd seen he addressed it.

'Do you feel better after speaking with Macey?'

'I do,' she said. 'I'm going to miss her.'

And I miss you, Candy thought, but she could not say that without starting to cry again.

'Could we go somewhere after work?' he said. 'Just to talk.'

She didn't really want to say goodbye to him here, not like this, so she nodded.

They returned to the café he had first taken her to, yet it felt so different now—the innocence and fun of before had left them.

'What would you like to eat?' he asked.

'I'll just have a cup of tea,' she said. 'I'm meeting my parents tonight.'

'Have you told them?'

Candy shook her head 'I'll tell them about the twins when I get back.'

'They'll know very soon.' He'd tried not to notice

her bump but now that he had he couldn't not see it. 'I'm not a very good doctor, am I?'

He somehow made her smile.

'I think it popped out about ten seconds after I found out...' Candy said. 'I'll just wear a big baggy top tonight. They're not talking to me anyway, because I changed the locks and I'm going to Hawaii, so I doubt I'll be there for very long.'

'Yet you still go.'

'I love them. I don't agree with them a lot of the time but I still love them very much and I know when I do tell them I'll break their hearts.'

'For a little while,' Steele said.

He took a breath. He could do this type of thing so easily for his patients but when it came to matters of a very private heart, things were very different, but he forced himself to step up.

'Would you like me to tell your parents for you?'

Candy frowned. 'Why would you do that?'

'Because I'm used to breaking news to difficult, stubborn, immutable people. I do it every day,' he said, and then made her smile. 'I promise to leave out the part that we've been at it like rabbits. I'll just say I'm a colleague. A doctor...'

Candy smiled. She really understood why he wore a suit and tie for work—the older people liked it. And he was right, her parents would respond very differently to Steele from the way they would to her. If not at first then fairly soon, they would calm down for the *dottore*.

'I need to do this myself, Steele. It's really nice of you to offer and I admit I'm tempted to pass it over, but...no. Thank you, though.'

'Is there anything I can do to help?'

'It's not your problem, Steele.' Then she looked over to him. 'Actually, this has helped and talking to Macey too. It makes it feel a bit more real.'

'Keep talking, then,' he said, but she shook her head.

'I can't really. I mean, I'm upset about Gerry too and I'm trying to work out how to tell his family and I don't think getting upset about Gerry is fair to you,' Candy said. 'I know I felt jealous when you spoke about your wife. I got an Annie burn.'

He loved her openness and he smiled when she admitted to having felt jealous. 'Candy, you *can* talk to me about that.' Ten years older, there were some things he did know. 'Two days before I turned thirty I found out that a woman who I had gone out with for close to six months, just after my divorce, had died. Now, she wasn't *the* love of my life. She was one of possibly too many *loves* of my life…' He saw her pale smile. 'And it hurt. I was stunned and devastated. I was all of the things that you probably are now.'

'It doesn't make you feel jealous when I talk about him?' Candy checked.

'I don't know how it makes me feel,' he admitted, touched that even with all that was going on in her world she could be concerned in that way for him. 'But that's my stuff to deal with. Right now you've got enough of your own.'

'Oh, I do!'

'You know there is one teeny positive,' Steele said.

'Tell me.'

'Well, there was one thing about you that was starting to get on my nerves, a potential deal-breaker, in fact,' Steele said. 'Confirmed bachelors are very picky and selfish, you understand…'

Candy smiled. 'Tell me.'

'Your ability to fall asleep. God, I knew you were tired, we both were, but I was starting to wonder if you had narcolepsy or something.'

She laughed but it changed in the middle and she fought from letting out a sob because he'd just reminded her how very good it had been between them.

'Candy…' He took her hand but she pulled hers away.

'Please, don't, Steele,' she said. They had always been honest and she was never more so than now. 'Please, don't confuse me now. I miss you very much. I think we both know that it was turning into a bit more than a fling. I think we both know that feelings were starting to run deep.' Which was milder than the complete truth but now was not the time to admit to love. She pointed out the impossibility of it.

'You like the single life.'

'I did,' he said, 'but I very much liked being with you.'

'You've geared your life around not having children.'

'I have,' he said.

'You start your dream job in a couple of weeks.'

'I do.'

'And I'm pregnant with another man's babies.'

It dawned on him then that he had only ever known Candy pregnant. That, really, nothing had changed between them, except that they both now knew and he told her so.

'Candy, since the moment we met you've been pregnant with another man's babies. I think we—'

'Steele,' she interrupted. 'I have to work a few things

out myself. I've been raised to share everything, to discuss every decision. I don't want to do that now. I want to think. I want to know that I can do this on my own. I have to know that I can do this on my own…'

'I get that.'

'And please don't pretend this isn't difficult for you.'

He thought back to that morning, sitting on the edge of the bath and crying in a way he never had before, but he felt better for it, clearer for it. He looked at Candy and knew she was right. She didn't need his thoughts now. She needed her holiday, she needed space, she needed to get used to the idea that she was going to be a mother.

'I need to go,' she said. She was on the edge of tears—just one touch of his hand and she wanted more, she wanted his arms, she wanted the comfort of him. She felt as if she had just got off a merry-go-round as they stepped outside. She had felt like that since the news about Gerry's death had hit, since she'd sat in Anton's office, since…

The world seemed to be spinning too fast of late, and Candy took a big breath and tried to steady herself, but big breaths seemed to be working less and less these days. Steele must have seen she was struggling. He wrapped her in his arms, as he had wanted to yesterday but hadn't known how. The shield of him, the feel of him, the tender strength of him brought the first glimpse of peace she had craved, just a tiny glimpse of tranquillity as solo she halted navigated stormy seas.

'You're going to be okay,' he said, and his voice was like the deep bass of a guitar coming up through the floorboards, a rhythm she recognised and understood, and she clung to the delicious familiarity of him and wished it could last. 'I know it's going to be hard, telling your parents, but when you do just remind them that this is their grandchildren they are discussing and that in few months they'll be here...'

'Right now I'm actually not worried about them,' she said. Right now she was wondering how she might ever get over this broken heart, but she daren't be that honest and so, for the first time, she lied to him. 'Right now I'm worried about stretch marks and my boobs reaching the moon and getting fatter...' *And losing you.* 'I'm going to go.'

Still he held her. 'I'll drive you home.'

Still she clung to him. 'I don't want you to.'

'I can drop off your case.'

She hated that he had it in his car.

Steele hated that it was in his car too. He wanted it in his apartment unpacked, he wanted her in his bed, yet he was terribly aware that he must not push her, not confuse her when she was already in such turmoil.

Maybe there was something he could do.

'Do you fancy a day pass?' he said to her ear.

'A day pass?'

'I'm going to Kent tomorrow to look at the new unit and also to look at a few houses that I'm thinking of buying...'

'You're buying a house?

'I always buy houses or flats wherever I work and I renovate them in my spare time and sell them or rent them out.'

'I'm working in Emergency tomorrow.'

'Oh, if anyone deserves to ring in sick, I think it might be you. Why don't we just have a nice drive, a lazy day...?'

'And no talk about pregnancy.'

'You don't have to pretend you're not pregnant, Candy.'

'I want a day away from it,' she admitted. 'I just want a whole day when I don't even have to think about it.'

'Then that's the day you shall have,' he said, and saw her to the Underground. 'I'll pick you up at eight.'

Candy sat on the tube, looking at all the people, and she saw an elderly woman look at her stomach and then her hand. She glanced up and saw that Candy had seen her and the old lady gave her a very nice smile.

Yes, times had changed.

She didn't feel quite so alone now.

It really was time to deal with what was.

Instead of heading home, she went to her parents'.

They were still sulking about Hawaii.

'Do you remember Gerry, who I work with?' Candy said. 'The one who helped me when I moved?'

'What about him?' Her father frowned. 'Is he going to Hawaii with you?'

'He died last week,' Candy said.

There were all the *How terribles* and Candy took a deep breath. She knew there was no easy way to say it.

It just needed to be said.

'I've just found out that I'm pregnant with twins,' Candy said. 'They're his.'

There were sobs and wails from her parents; her mother actually fell to the floor. As if that was going to change anything!

She had never understood Steele more than she did then. She understood fully how his love for Annie might have died as she watched her parents carry on.

This was about her, this was the hardest part of her life to date, and yet they made it all about them.

She had known they'd be upset but, as Steele would say, that was their stuff. How Candy wished they could give some teeny shred of comfort as she tried to deal with hers.

Candy sat there as her father declared he'd like to kill the man who had taken his daughter's honour and then she stood up.

'Lui è già morto,' Candy said, reminding her father that Gerry was already dead, and then she remembered Steele's words.

'These are your grandchildren we're discussing.' Her voice was incredibly clear and strong. 'And these are my babies and I refuse to listen to you calling them a mistake or talking about shame. In a few months they'll be here and you know as well as I do that you're going to love them. So why do this to me now? I'm going to go and I don't want to hear from you till you've calmed down.' She went to the door. 'And if you want to come to my flat, then you're to telephone before you do. Clearly I have a life you don't know about, and if you still don't want to know about it, then you're to telephone first before you come around!'

She left her parents and she could perhaps have headed for home but instead she did as Steele had once suggested she try.

She bought a single ticket for a movie—the one they hadn't seen that night. It was a real tear-jerker from start to end and she sat there, tears pouring down her face and not trying to hide them.

It was nice, a tiny press of the pause button as she

cried over the couple on the screen instead of dwelling on herself.

On Steele.

On what could surely never be.

CHAPTER TWELVE

HER JEANS JUST did up.

Nervous and a little excited, just as she had been the first time he'd come to her door, she opened it the next morning with a smile.

'I'm ready,' she said, 'or did you want a drink first?'

'No, thanks,' Steele said. 'It's probably better that we get going. I've got a lot to get on with today.' He couldn't not comment. 'You've been crying.'

'I had a rather big argument with my parents last night.'

'You told them?'

'I did.' She blew out a breath. 'And I told them a few other things too. Anyway, we're not talking about all that stuff today. I really do want a day off from it.'

'Fair enough.' He smiled. 'But can I just say that I'm really proud of you for telling them.'

'Thank you.'

'You'll enjoy your holiday far more without that hanging over you.'

'I shall.'

They went out to his car and were soon on the motorway. 'First up,' Steele explained, 'I'm going to look at the new wing of the hospital, which might bore the hell out of you. You can go for a walk or to the shops if you like.'

'No, I'd love to see it,' Candy said, 'unless explaining me makes things awkward for you.'

'I never feel the need to explain myself,' he said, and then he amended that slightly. 'Actually, I did cancel dinner with my parents tonight, you would have taken some explaining.'

'Oh, sorry,' Candy said, 'I didn't want you to change your plans for me.'

'I was more than happy to change them. I'm moving closer to them in a few weeks.' He turned and smiled again. 'Though not quite close as you are to yours, but they'll be seeing more of me than they do now.'

'What are they like now?'

'They've mellowed,' Steele said. 'They're much nicer as old people. Though I have to admit that when they start asking questions about my life, my love life, I'm often tempted to tell them to back off, given that they showed little interest in me when I was growing up.' He gave a roll of his eyes. 'I wouldn't do that to them, though.'

Candy knew that he wouldn't. He was too nice.

'You like old people.'

'I do,' he said. 'I don't like *all* old people. It's not a free pass to being a good person but I like how they've let go of the stuff that's not important. I like how they say what they think and share what they know. I like it even when my patients drive me mad with their stubbornness. I learn something every day, every single day, from how to put a brass doorknob on a house I'm renovating to how to face death.'

They arrived at the hospital and Steele shook hands

and introduced her to Reece, a consultant who'd clearly had a lot of input into the new wing.

'Any chance of you starting sooner?' Reece joked. 'Emergency is full.'

'No chance.' Steele smiled. 'I don't need you to show me around if you're busy.'

'You're sure?'

'Of course.'

'I'll see you at the meeting, then.' Reece nodded. 'Make sure you put a hard hat on.'

'I feel like a builder,' Candy said as she put hers on.

'Come on, Bob,' Steele said, and he took her through the building. It was near complete in parts and the roof was going on in others. 'This is going to be the acute geriatric unit,' he explained as he showed her a huge area where the wiring was going in. 'Very high-tech computer system,' he said. 'It has its own occupational therapy assessment area.' He took her in. There were two kitchens and various sets of stairs being built, as well as showers and baths of various heights so that patients could be assessed on how they would manage at home. 'I'm aiming for a forty-eight-hour admission time. Either home afterwards with support or admitted to the correct ward, but most of my patients will first come through here—well, that's the plan.'

'Forty-eight hours isn't very long.'

'Best time frame,' Steele said. 'It gives us enough time to put proper support in place for when they return to their homes.'

Steele showed her the other wards—a palliative care ward and also the acute medical unit—and then he opened a door and they stood in a huge empty space.

'This is the dream,' he said. 'It's not happening yet.

We're facing lots of obstacles and red tape, insurance issues and things, but I'm hoping this space will be a gym.' He smiled. 'Actually, I'm not allowed to call it that. I'm hoping this space will be utilised for healthy living...'

'Sorry?'

'Well, I always feel a bit of a bastard when I know someone's lonely and that a cream cake at three in the afternoon means not only a cream cake but a walk to the shops and some conversation too. Instead of asking them to give it up, I'm hoping that they can come here and have a chat with friends and maybe a bit of exercise. I'm hoping for a slimming or exercise club or something like that. It's all a bit of a pipe dream at the moment, but at least we have the space earmarked for it, if we ever do get to go ahead.'

'How long's your contract for?' Candy asked.

'Two years,' he said. 'They wanted five but I wouldn't agree to it.'

'Because?'

'Because I've never stayed anywhere for more than two years. I like fresh starts. I like putting everything into it and building things up...'

Or rather he had.

They drove to a pub and had a lovely lazy lunch overlooking a huge village green.

'Gorgeous, isn't it?' Candy said, and he nodded.

'Even if we don't get the go-ahead for the gym, I'll probably start a walking club over there.'

'You're going to go start a geriatric walking club!'

'Yep, I walk with my dog every morning that I can. Why not have company?'

'You have a dog?'

'I do.' Steele smiled. 'You have me pegged as a loner—no friends to go to the movies with, no pets. I have a dog, I have nice furniture and I have, when I'm not sleeping with Nurse Candy, a very busy social life.'

'Where's your dog now?'

'At my parents',' he said. 'He's a chocolate Labrador called Newman.'

'Newman?'

'You'll…' Steele stopped. He had been about to say she would see why when she met him but that wasn't what today was about. *No pressure*, he reminded himself. Today was doing her good, he could see that already. Her cheeks were pink and she seemed more relaxed than she had since…well, since Macey had opened her mouth and knocked their worlds off their axes, but they were starting to spin again, tentatively, though. 'He's got blue eyes,' Steele said instead. 'And he's the love of my life and he knows it.'

'Does he sleep on your bed, Steele?'

Steele shook his head. 'He sleeps on his bed for about seventeen hours a day and graciously lets me share it at night.'

After lunch they walked across the green and Candy laughed as she looked at it through what she imagined were Steele's eyes. 'I have this vision of all these old people doing Tai Chi…'

'So do I.'

She stopped walking. 'And then you'll leave.'

'That was the plan,' he said. 'Though this is a huge project…' He looked around. Since his divorce he had never been able to imagine staying in one place for very long. Here, though, he was close, though not too close to his parents; here was the job he had been working towards his entire career. He looked over as a car pulled up and a man got out and gave them a wave as they walked over to him.

'That's the estate agent,' Steele explained.

'Oh.'

'And that's the renovator's delight I'm hoping to buy, but I'm not telling him that.'

It was a huge rambling house with a small wooden gate, overlooking the green.

'Are you going to come and take a look?' he said.

'I think I might just take another walk,' she said. She didn't want to see his future home, so she walked on the green as Steele inspected the house.

He looked at the cornices and the hanging-off doors; the windows would all need to be taken out.

Don't start on the electrics, he thought as he flicked lights on and off.

And as for the plumbing! The estate agent tried to distract him from turning on taps but Steele was not easily distracted and when he turned on the taps the whole house seemed to rattle. Steele grinned as, in his head, he knocked another five grand off the asking price.

It was magnificent, though.

'Could you give me a moment?' he said to the agent. 'I'd like to walk through it again on my own for a minute.'

The estate agent agreed and Steele took way more than a minute.

The last time he had looked at a home this size had been with his ex-wife. The natural assumption at that time had been that the bedrooms would soon be filled.

The natural assumption as he walked around now was that the bedrooms would be filled too.

It was more than an assumption. It was a feeling it was how it should be. He looked out of a window and could see Candy idly walking around. He wanted to go and fetch her, bring her in, ask her her thoughts, yet her thoughts were cluttered enough now.

His weren't.

He thanked the estate agent and said that he'd be in touch then he walked over and joined her.

'Maybe I can explain you after all,' he said.

'Sorry?'

'I could just say to my parents that you're a friend from work who needed a day out. You can meet Newman.'

'No, thanks,' she said.

'Candy, can we talk—'

'Please, not now,' she said. 'I just need this day. I just need a day of not dealing with it and then I need my holiday to start dealing with it on my own.'

Steele nodded. It was what they had agreed to after all.

They drove back to his flat to collect her case, which was no longer in the car, and Candy needed it as she flew tomorrow.

Candy, of course, fell asleep in the car but now it just made him smile.

She awoke to his lovely deep voice and the sight of his flat and then she turned and there he was.

'I'll go and grab your case,' he said.

'Can I borrow your loo?' Candy said, because, as she was starting to find out, this was something she would be saying rather a lot in the weeks and months ahead.

She went to the loo and remembered the last time she'd been here—when her pregnancy had just started to become a possibility. As she looked in the mirror while washing her hands, she remembered the fear that had been in her eyes then.

The fear was gone now.

Yes, she was confused and exhausted and nervous about how she would provide for two children, but the terror was leaving and, after such a wonderful day's reprieve, she was starting to feel a little more like herself.

'Thank you for a lovely day,' she said.

'Do you want a cup of tea?' he offered, and she nodded.

'Make yourself comfortable.'

'Ha-ha,' she said, and stood and watched him make the tea instead.

Meaning…

She lifted her top and showed him the straining zipper that had simply refused to go all the way back up.

Only Steele didn't really see that. He saw pink lace and a teeny flash of jet hair and the stomach that his mouth had kissed over and over.

And as she put down her top Candy looked at the teabag he was squeezing the hell out of with his spoon and, yikes, there was a sort of gravelly note to his voice as he asked her how many sugars she had in her tea.

'The same as last time,' Candy said.

'Sorry, I'm a bit distracted.' Steele smiled. 'Two?'

'Two.'

'Do you really want tea?' he checked.

'No.'

'Because I don't,' Steele said. 'I want a glass of wine but I'm driving.'

'Poor Steele.' She smiled. 'It really is a problem.' Candy thought for a moment. 'I know!' she said brightly.

'Do tell.'

'Why don't you have a glass of wine and drive me home later?'

He turned and faced her. 'That's so clever, but you're stuck in those uncomfortable jeans. I insist you take them off...'

They started to kiss, the best kiss ever, because she'd got so lost in babies and feeling massive and unsexy but his tongue swiftly took care of that.

It hadn't really entered her head that he might want her again in that way. Now his fingers were at her zipper and somehow she felt back to the woman she had been.

Out of her jeans, she moaned in relief.

'Nice?'

'Nice,' she said to his mouth.

'That bra looks a bit tight too.'

He unhooked it and took it out through her arms and it was lovely to be all loose and floppy and to rest a moment in his arms.

'Feels so good,' she said.

'It does,' he said. There would be no rushing. He loved feeling her all relaxed against him.

'Get your wine.'

They headed over to the sofa and it was nice to be back there. Steele sat and Candy lay down as he drank his wine and played with her hair. It was good not to talk. She remembered the mornings with Macey and her *nonna*, and the bliss of hush when words could only serve to make you sad.

'Are you all packed for Hawaii?' he said finally.

'Nope.' Candy sighed. 'We're here to get my case, remember?'

This time tomorrow she'd be at Heathrow.

'Can I paint your toenails?' she asked.

'Er, why?'

'It relaxes me and my mum's still sulking at me so I haven't been able to do hers.'

'Do you have some nail varnish with you?'

'In my bag.'

He was so laid back and yet so austere. It was a lovely mixture that made her stomach curl and also gave her a peace that she could be herself.

And she was.

He lay down and she sat on his calves and started on his right foot. 'I like men's nails,' Candy explained, 'because they're bigger.'

'Have you painted a lot of men's nails?' he asked, and then let out a moan of surprise. 'Oh!'

'What?' She smiled as she painted his big toenail.

'I have nail-painting jealousy issues,' Steele said. 'I just felt it burn. I'm looking at your bum and enjoying the view when I suddenly got the Annie burn that you had.'

'I've never painted another man's toenails from this angle.' Candy smiled again.

'Take your knickers off, then.'

She did as told and then got back to painting the toenails on his left foot but she made a terrible mess of his long second toe because she heard his zipper slide down.

'I'm making a bit of a mess here, Steele,' she said.

'I forgive you,' he said.

'Steele.' She was arguably the most turned on she had ever been. She had never thought she'd feel sexy again, had never thought sex would ever be fun again, and yet here they were and it was bliss. 'Can I turn around?'

'You'll finish what you started,' Steele warned.

She gritted her teeth and did the last three toes really quickly. 'Done.' She turned around on his calves to the delicious sight of him and she moved up to sit on his thighs and lowered her head and they shared a long, deep kiss. Her breasts flattened against his chest and she could feel his erection pressing against her stomach.

She brought the kiss to a giddy halt and stared at him. He looked right back at her in a way that had her almost feverish. She started placing small kisses over his cheeks as his hands moved to her breasts, working her nipples.

'Candy...' Steele nearly said something he shouldn't. Today wasn't a day for confusing her, today wasn't a day for declarations, it was about keeping it light and he felt her sudden tension at the tender tone to his voice. 'Time for your hula lesson,' he said, and got the reward of her laugh in his ear.

She lowered herself onto him and he held her hips and had her sway a little and circle, and then Candy could not play any longer and she started moving of her own accord. His hands exploring her breasts had her greedy for more and she leant forward, lowering her breasts to his mouth, dizzy with the sensation of his hands now on her hips, grinding her down a little harder as his mouth worked her tender nipples.

'Steele...' There was almost panic in her voice, a delicious panic because her body wasn't hers any more but was moving into a rhythm of its own.

His mouth left her breast and she looked down at him. His lips were slightly parted and there was tension in his expression, just as there was in hers.

Steele adjusted the angle of his thrust just a fraction and she let out a sob. It was an actual sob as Steele started to come.

And then another sob and it was one of relief as somehow, some way, as she came to him, all she was at that moment was Candy.

Not pregnant, not scared, not worried at all.

The world felt a lot better when she was in Steele's arms.

CHAPTER THIRTEEN

STEELE STARED AT the morning light as she lay in his arms.

It was the last morning they would share in this room.

'Excited?'

'Very.' Candy nodded.

Despite her misgivings at times, now she was looking forward again to going on holiday. There was so much more to sort out now and Candy truly wanted to get on with it.

Right now, though, here was where she wanted to be, and she lay stroking the crinkly hair on his stomach that she loved so.

'What date do you get back?' Steele asked.

It was the first day of his new job.

'Do you want me to see if I can get away this evening and take you to the airport?'

'No, because then we'll have to say goodbye again.' She looked up at him. He'd been so lovely to her. Her time with Steele had been the most wonderful time of her life but she wasn't foolish. Two weeks away from each other, him starting a new job, very soon he might look at things in a very different light. She didn't want to find out a few weeks or months from now that, despite best intentions, they hadn't worked out... A very big part of Candy wanted it left at this. She wanted it to end while they were crazy about each other, while it was fun and sex and romance—before it all got too hard.

They got out of bed and got ready and he picked up her case and when they got to her flat he carried it in and he laughed when he saw the lock she'd put on.

'How many holes did you put in the door?'

'I'm very proud of my work,' Candy said.

'I'm not sure your landlord will be,' Steele said, and smiled as Candy went a bit pink. 'Did you ask permission?'

'No.'

'Do you want me to fix it up?'

'No,' she said. 'I want to fix it myself.'

'I know you do.'

They had a cuddle in the hall, a quiet one, just stood there and held each other and the moment was theirs.

He drove her to work and as they went to say good-bye it was too hard to do. 'I'll pop in and see Macey and if you're on the ward...'

'Sure.'

He gave her a kiss and they both did their very best to get on with their day.

'Candy...' Kelly said as she came into the changing room. 'How are things?'

'Sorry?'

'You were off sick yesterday,' Kelly fished.

'I wasn't sick, though.' Candy smiled. 'It was a mental health day.'

'So everything is okay?' Kelly checked.

'It will be about ten hours from now when my plane takes off.' She knew Kelly was fishing—everyone was.

And at midday Candy broke her news as they dealt with a multi-trauma.

'I'm stepping out,' she said as they went to do the X-rays. She always wore a heavy lead gown and so she knew it would not have affected the twins, but she just chose to let people know then. 'I'm pregnant, so I'd rather not take the chance…'

She left the room and let out a breath. Steele was right, she'd enjoy her holiday much more without that hanging over her.

And she dealt with the second question on everyone's minds as she stepped back in.

'I'm not comfortable yet discussing who the father is, but you'll all be very excited to know I'm expecting twins.'

There were smiles and congratulations and even a bottle of iced lemonade to toast her at the end of her shift.

'Have fun!' Lydia said. 'Lots of it.'

'Oh, I shall.'

She headed up to the geriatric unit and said goodbye to a couple of patients before she got to her very favourite one.

'Enjoy yourself,' Macey said. 'You deserve to be happy. A rather clever doctor told me that.'

Candy nodded. She had every intention of being happy, but as she gave Macey a cuddle and said goodbye she asked a question, desperate for the older woman's sage thoughts.

'Macey,' Candy said carefully. 'I want to be happy but what if you're not certain that the other person truly is? What if they might be there only out of a sense of duty?'

'Duty?' Macey thought for a long moment and Candy realised she was holding her breath as she awaited her answer, but Macey clearly didn't quite understand her question. 'Duty to who?' Macey asked.

'It doesn't matter,' Candy said, and gave her a smile. 'Stay well and I shall send you a postcard.'

As she left Macey she saw Steele going into his office and she went and knocked at the door.

'Are you off?'

'I am,' Candy said. 'Well, I've just got to see the obstetrician, buy a bikini, pack, take the Underground...'

'You're sure you don't want me to take you?'

'I'm very sure,' she said, and he took her in his arms. 'Thank you,' Candy said. 'I know we only had a short time and I know it was a bit fraught but you really helped and I just...' She couldn't really finish saying what she wanted to say without crying. 'I might write to you,' she said. 'Or call you. I really don't know...'

'You stop worrying about me and just go and have a wonderful time,' he said. 'Do what you have to do. Oh, one thing...' He took out his wallet and peeled off some US dollars.

'Stop!' Candy said. 'I don't need a sugar daddy.'

'I'm not old enough to be your sugar daddy.' He laughed. 'Seriously, I've had these for about five years, since my last trip to the States. Have fun with it.'

'Thank you!' Candy smiled.

'Go,' he said.

'But—'

'Go,' he said again, and she was glad that he did

because she wanted to say goodbye smiling and if she stayed a moment longer she might possibly cry.

Then it was time for her official appointment with Anton.

'I told you that you were about to start showing,' he said with a smile as she walked in. 'Have people started noticing?'

'Yes, though no one had the nerve to ask if I was pregnant just yet, though a patient told me that I was before I even knew. I've just announced it. I also said that I'm not comfortable with telling them who the father is.'

'Well done.' Anton smiled again.

He checked her blood pressure and all was well then Candy climbed up onto the examination table and he spoke to her about twin pregnancies. He said her babies would probably be born at around thirty-seven weeks and that he would see her more regularly than he would for a singleton pregnancy.

'Have you told your parents?'

Candy nodded. 'They didn't take it very well at all.'

'They'll come around.'

'I know,' she said. 'I told them to contact me when they do. I think I'm going to tell Gerry's parents when I return from my holiday. I think that it is only fair to them to know.'

'What about your new partner?'

'He's not really my partner, I don't think,' Candy said as Anton helped her to sit up. 'It was supposed to be just casual thing. He starts a new job soon and is moving. He'll be gone by the time I get back from my holiday. I don't know what will happen then, if anything.' She smiled at Anton. 'My bad for falling in love.'

'You have told the insurance companies that you're pregnant?'

'I have.'

'Go and have and amazing holiday. Grieve, cry, smile and heal.'

'Thank you.'

They sounded like pretty straightforward instructions and as she packed the last few pieces into her suitcase she called for a taxi to take her to the Underground.

Usually her parents would go with her to the airport to wave her off as if she were going on an expedition for a year but they were clearly not over the news yet so Candy took the Underground and battled with evening commuters and her suitcase.

She caught sight of a pregnant woman's reflection in the window and it took a second before she realised that it was her own.

We'll get there, she said in her mind to her small bump. She loved them already. The numb shock had worn off. The fear had gone. Already Candy knew she'd cope.

They would get through this.

As she checked in at Heathrow and watched her case shoot away she turned and saw her parents.

'Ma...' Candy ran over and hugged them.

'We love you.'

'I know you do.'

'We'll help.'

'I know you will,' Candy said, and they kissed and made up with much relief.

'You move from that flat and come home,' her mother said. 'We can help you to raise them—'

'We'll talk when I get home,' Candy said. 'Thank you so much for coming to the airport. It means an awful lot to me.'

It had but as she sat on the plane she knew she was moving from her flat but not to her parents' home.

She thought of Steele raised by his grandmother. No, she didn't want that for the twins. She wanted to raise her children herself, her way, and not her parents' way.

There was so much to sort out, so very much, but as she disembarked from the plane nearly a day later and a lei was placed around her neck Candy was the happiest tourist on the planet and knew Hawaii was the right place to be.

'Aloha,' a gorgeous woman said.

Yes, she was happy, yet that evening as she walked along the beach, how she wished Steele was here beside her—dipping his red toenails in the Pacific, making her laugh, making her smile, letting her be who she was.

Candy loved the way he accepted her just as she was.

CHAPTER FOURTEEN

'ARE YOU GOING to a funeral?' Macey checked, seeing Steele's dark suit and tie the following Tuesday morning. 'Wait till you get to my age. I go to one a month.'

'It's a memorial service,' he said. He really liked speaking with Macey. She was so blunt about everything.

'Oh, is it for that nurse in Emergency?' she asked. 'The one Elaine's crying over?'

'Elaine?' Steele glanced across the ward and sure enough a very flat Elaine, very un-bossy of late Elaine, was sitting at the desk when she'd normally be bustling about. 'He got off with her at a Christmas party,' Macey said, 'from what I can make out. Then he had nothing to do with her the next day. I would say he wasn't a good caretaker of lovely young hearts.'

'Oh, he's St Gerry now.' Steele rolled his eyes.

'And I shall be St Macey for a while after I die and then people will start to remember what a cantankerous old thing I really was.'

He laughed and looked into her wise eyes. 'You don't miss anything, do you?'

'Not with the new medication.' She smiled. 'I'm back.'

'God help us, then.' Steele smiled.

'You wouldn't have met him, though,' Macey said, and the smile was wiped off his face at her perception.

'Sorry?'

'He was in Greece, had been there a couple of months when it happened, well, according to the porter who took me for my X-ray... That's what he said to the radiographer anyway.'

'I believe so.'

'So why are you going to his memorial service if you never met?'

Steele said nothing, just gave Macey a small nod and walked off.

He sat at the desk and tried to write notes, but he ached. He actually ached sitting there.

He missed Candy, more than he had ever missed anyone.

He'd never missed anybody really, apart from his grandmother when she'd died.

It felt like grief. It really did.

It was grief because he missed her. He even missed the bump of her twins, or was he just imagining that?

He pulled up his emails and looked at the image of Gerry and it wasn't jealousy he was feeling. Steele understood that now.

It was guilt.

Guilt because this young man had died. Guilt that he might be swooping in and raising his babies because he couldn't have any of his own.

Steele let out a breath and then jumped slightly as a voice startled him.

'I'm here to see Macey Anderson...' Steele glanced

up and saw a good-looking middle-aged man wearing a suit and tie and carrying a huge bunch of flowers.

He was nervous, he was anxious and he was hers, Steele knew.

'I'll take you over.' He stood and as they walked to the bed he would never forget the small cry of recognition that escaped Macey as she looked down the ward and for the first time saw her son.

He ran to her.

Those last two steps he actually ran and Steele pulled the curtains around them as Macey held her fifty-five-year-old baby for the very first time.

Some things were private but Steele knew he'd just witnessed love.

Steele checked in on Macey a couple of hours later. She had gone to bed for a lie down, but he found her sitting up, smiling, with a huge bunch of flowers beside her bed and a photo album that her son had brought for her.

'I'm a grandmother,' she said, showing Steele a photo. 'And in two weeks I'll be a great-grandmother. He was a bit worried about telling me that.' Macey gave a delighted smile. 'His daughter, Samantha, is only eighteen. They're coming to visit me when I'm home.'

'You're going to be busy, Macey,' Steele said.

'I shall be. I'd say I'm going to have to hang around for a while yet.' She looked at him. 'Do you know, I always worried what sort of home he'd gone to, more than I worried about what he thought of me. He was raised beautifully. They loved him from the moment they got him and still do… It's a huge weight off my mind.'

'I'm very glad,' he said, and then he moved to go because she was cutting a bit close to the bone.

'I wondered if they'd love him as their own,' Macey said. 'I wondered if he'd resent them if he found out he wasn't biologically theirs, but they were just so open about it…'

'I'm very pleased to hear that,' Steele responded. 'Now, if you'll excuse me, I have to go.'

As he went to do that Macey's words stopped him.

'So she's in Hawaii…'

'Sorry?' he said, and turned.

Macey gave him an odd look. 'Are we going to pretend that you don't know who I'm talking about?'

'I don't,' Steele said.

'Do you think you stop being a matron? I used to know everything that went on in my department. Do you really think I just lie here?'

Steele had never had anyone meddle in his love life, or lack of a love life, and he wasn't going to start now. 'I have to go, Macey.'

'You just interrupted me, Doctor. Why is she in Hawaii and you're here?'

'I don't discuss my private life…'

'But you're fine with me discussing mine?'

'You're my job,' Steele said to her, but she just smiled at him.

'And you're hard work!' she said. 'You're certainly not so chipper these days.'

'I apologise,' he said. 'I shouldn't bring my problems to work with me.'

'How are *you*, Steele?' she said. 'And that's Matron asking.'

Steele remembered Candy sitting here, crying, on this very bed. It had been Macey who had told them both that Candy was pregnant after all. He sat on the bed and this time he was there for himself rather than Macey and he told her how he felt.

'Sad.'

'I'm sorry.'

'I miss her.'

'You don't have to miss her, though.'

'She needs this break.'

'Perhaps, but she'll come back and you'll be gone, living miles away, immersed in your new job. That's not the start that you two need.'

'She needs time to think.'

'Of course she does,' Macey said, 'but you can have too much time and get yourself into a space that it's very hard to get out of.'

She was right. Steele knew that. Of course, Candy's parents would soon come round. From the little he knew about them, he knew that they loved their daughter. They would want to help. They would probably suggest that she move back in with them. He thought about trying to forge a relationship with her parents as gatekeepers.

They didn't need to forge anything, Steele realised.

He didn't need to question himself about his motives towards the pregnancy.

He loved her.

It was that easy.

Macey watched the smile that spread on his face and, yes, some things were private but she knew too that she'd just witnessed the realisation of love.

Steele sat through the long memorial service and heard what an amazing man St Gerry had been, but it didn't hurt him now.

Indeed, he could laugh at a few of his antics.

By all accounts he had been a bit wild, a bit bold, and now, as the shock of his death started to recede, the real Gerry started to appear.

They all stood as his parents cut a ribbon for the new resuscitation ward and everybody headed up towards Admin for drinks and nibbles and more talk about Gerry, but Steele chose not to go there.

'Steele!' Hugh, a surgeon he had asked to consult on a patient, came over and shook his hand. 'Have you met Rory?'

'I have.' He shook Rory's hand.

'And this is Gina. She's also an anaesthetist here,' Hugh introduced, but Steele couldn't place her.

'I *used* to be an anaesthetist here,' Gina said.

'It's lovely to meet you,' he said, and then watched Gina's features tighten as a man made his way over.

'This is Anton,' Hugh said, and Steele shook Anton's hand as Hugh introduced them. 'Anton's an obstetrician.'

'Well,' Steele said, 'that would explain why we haven't met. We don't have much call for obstetricians on the geriatric unit.'

'I'm also a reproductive specialist,' Anton said. 'Though I guess you don't have much call up there for them either.' He turned to Hugh. 'Are you going up to Admin for drinks?'

'No.' Hugh shook his head. 'I've got to get back to Theatre. Anyway, I've done my duty and put in an appearance but, frankly, he was an arrogant piece of work and I had more arguments with him than anyone else at the Royal.'

Anton watched as Steele gave a wry smile.

'Well, I certainly don't need to be around booze,' Gina said. 'I'm heading for home. I might see you around.' She smiled at Steele. 'I've got an interview next week.'

'Good luck,' Steele said.

Anton, he noticed, made no comment.

Gina walked off and there was an uncomfortable silence for a moment.

'How is she?' Hugh asked Rory.

'How would I know?' Rory said. 'We're not really talking any more.'

The two men walked off, leaving just Steele and Anton.

'Undercurrents?' Steele checked, because around Gina things had seemed incredibly tense.

'Hell, yes,' Anton said, but didn't elaborate. 'I think I might give the drinks in Admin a miss too, although I could use a drink. Do you want to go over to Imelda's?' he offered. Imelda's was a bar across from the hospital and Steele nodded.

'Sure.'

'Have you worked here long?' Steele asked as they gave their orders a few minutes later.

'Just over a year,' Anton said. 'You?'

'I'm only here for a few more weeks. I move to Kent the week after next.'

'My first intention was to be here for a couple of years and then return to Milan, but my wife works here and she's pregnant. I can't see me leaving here any time soon.'

'You said that you worked in fertility?'

'That's right.'

'Is it hard to do both?' Steele asked.

'I set firm boundaries,' Anton explained. 'I first did obstetrics then moved into fertility. I missed it, though, and so when I moved to England I changed back to obstetrics. I still keep my hand in when I can. I would love somehow to do both but they are both very consuming.'

'There are a lot of changes, I guess?' Steele could not believe he was pushing this conversation.

Anton could. 'There are constant changes.'

'What about for men?' Steele asked. 'I mean, you hear all the advancements for women...' He could not believe he was discussing this. He actually wanted to stop because if there wasn't hope then perhaps it would be better not to know.

'Things are different for men also. There is a pro-cedure called ICSE now. Basically, if you can get one healthy sperm an egg can be fertilised. Even if the sperm count comes back as negative, you can go into the vas deferens...'

Steele pulled a face at the thought of a needle in his balls.

'Under local.' Anton smiled.

He'd do it.

And there was the difference, Steele realised. He'd had a lot of loves in his life but never till now 'the one'.

One that meant two hours after taking his first sip of a very welcome Scotch and a whole lot of talking with Anton, he was standing in a room, pants around his ankles, filling a specimen jar.

'That was quick,' Anton teased as Steele came into his office and he took the jar. 'You might want to work on that.' Then he was serious as he prepared the sample. 'You know that if I find nothing in the specimen I can still go into the vas deferens. I might want to do that sober, though.'

'Just tell me.'

CHAPTER FIFTEEN

CANDY CRIED OVER GERRY.

And on days two and three Candy cried quite a bit about finding herself twenty-four years old and pregnant with twins.

Day three she had explored the island and on day four the dam broke and Candy sobbed at the unfairness of it all, that the man she knew she loved had arrived in her life at a time when all the odds were stacked against them.

By day five she gave up on crying and took Steele's money, which she had in a separate purse, and bought a fabulous, seriously fabulous sea-green sarong.

As she handed over the money it felt crinkly and new and she glanced at it and she started laughing.

Liar, liar.

These were far newer notes than Steele had said they were.

He had been to the bank after all!

She loved him.

A lot more relaxed and a little bit sunburnt, in the late afternoon Candy put on her sarong and set off. She sat on a hill, looking out at the ocean, and tried to finally sort her list out.

She dealt with the easiest first.

Job.

She chewed her pen for a full two minutes before deciding that she did love Emergency. No, she didn't want them all finding out that the twins were Gerry's but, of course, they would.

And she'd deal with it.

The Gerry's Wing thing was a bit *ouch*, but she'd just have to suck it up.

She needed the maternity leave.

Which brought her onto the next thing that was worrying her—money. She didn't write that down. Candy didn't even have to think about that. She wrote 'Ha-ha-ha' instead and then moved on to the next one.

Gerry's parents.

Okay, she would telephone them when she returned and tell them the news and, if they wanted to or when they'd calmed down, she would offer to go and speak with them.

Next.

Her parents.

Candy had already decided she was moving, far away so that they couldn't just drop in. Even if it would be easier to have them nearer.

She took a breath. The harder matters were approaching.

Gerry.

'I should have gone to the memorial service.'

Candy didn't know what else to write. She didn't know how to write that she didn't love him but she hated that he was dead and that not only would the world move on without him, but he would have children and not know.

They would know about him though, Candy promised.

'I will tell the twins about you and keep in touch with your family.'

And then she got to the top of the list but she'd left it till last because it was the one that left her so, so confused.

Steele.

She could write to him perhaps. Maybe it would be better in a letter. But telling someone you loved them when you were pregnant with someone else's children came at a huge disadvantage and it was an impossible letter to write.

She never wanted him to think that she wanted him simply as a father for her children.

The natural order of falling in love had for the most part been denied them.

She tried to keep it light, wondering through her words that if it was all too much to deal with for him, maybe they could somehow be friends with benefits. Then she screwed up that piece of paper because given how much her stomach had grown in the past few days she doubted if very soon she would appeal to him.

And so she wrote him a postcard—one she had swiped from the villa and had meant to use for Macey.

Steele,
I wish...how I wish...that you were here now.
Candy xxx

List sorted, she decided.

Now she had to get on with relaxing.

As she walked back she thought she was seeing

things because there, sitting on the little chair outside her villa, was Steele. He was wearing dark jeans and a black T-shirt and was very unshaven but very welcome to her eyes.

'I didn't know I had a genie.' She met him with a smile.

This was how he remembered her, Steele thought as she approached. This was how she'd been before it had all happened—here she was smiling, laughing, intuitive and sexy. She handed him the postcard she had written and he read it with a smile.

'That explains what happened, then,' Steele said. 'One minute I was sitting chatting to Macey and the next, *puff*, here I was in Hawaii…' He looked at her and took in the changes, and not just to her body.

She had been right to come alone, he conceded, because it had served her well—she looked relaxed and healthy and happy.

It was very nice to see.

'I've been making lists,' Candy said. 'I'm all sorted now.'

'Can I see?' he asked, and then shook his head. 'Sorry, stupid thing to ask.'

'Go for it,' she said.

'Let's go for a walk,' he said, and he dropped his bag in the villa and took her hand. They headed to the beach and sat there.

She could hear the wind through the palm trees and was all knotted on the inside but in a very nice way.

Steele was here.

'Why are you here?' she asked.

'Because I had this vision of trying to date you from

Kent while you were living with your parents,' Steele said as he read through her list.

'I'd already addressed that,' she said, and pointed to her decision on the list she had written.

So she had.

'I feel like the teacher is reading my homework,' she admitted. 'Do I get marked?'

'Verbal comments,' Steele said. 'I didn't bring my red pen.

'Okay, I think moving away from your parents is very brave and very sensible.'

'Thank you.'

'And I think telling Gerry's parents is very brave and very right too,' Steele said, and carried on reading through her list.

'Work...' Steele said, and his hand wavered in the air. 'That's a tough one.'

'I like what I do.'

'I know.

'What's "Ha-ha-ha" for?'

'Money,' Candy said, and he laughed.

He was serious when they got to Gerry. 'As for the memorial service...'

'I feel bad that I didn't go.'

'I went,' Steele said.

'Were there a lot of people?'

'It was packed,' he said. He decided not to mention Elaine and her tears. He had spoken to her the next day and had hopefully helped by listening a bit.

'I met Rory, and Gina...'

'Gina!' Candy's eyes were wide. 'She's been on extended leave. I think she's been in rehab.'

'Well, it looks as if she's coming back,' Steele said.

'Oh, and I met Anton. We went for a drink afterwards.' He watched as she blushed. 'Is he the doctor overseeing your pregnancy?'

'Yes.'

'Did you happen to mention my infertility?'

'I did.'

'It's fine that you told him. I don't have any issue with that at all. You must have been in the most confused space.'

'So how did you guess that he was my doctor?'

'Heathrow to Hawaii gives you quite a lot of thinking time.' He told her all the questions he'd had for Anton and then he told her why. 'I'm here because I love you, but I never wanted you to think I wanted you for the babies. Does that make sense?'

'Sort of.'

'Anyway, I'm not. I want the babies very much but if it hadn't happened, it helps to know that you very probably can have a baby with me. Not naturally, but the choice and the chance is there.'

She turned and smiled at him. 'Did you do it into a jar for me?'

'I did,' he said. 'And, had it been necessary, I would have undergone a procedure that would involve a lot of local anaesthetic on a very delicate area but, thankfully, Anton seems to think I've got enough swimmers to work with.'

'You asked Anton all those embarrassing questions for me?'

'Yes.' Steele sighed. 'I did. I had no idea at the time that Anton had practically led me to ask them—you've got a lot of fans, you know.'

'Who?'

'Anton, Macey...'

'How is Macey?'

'Meddling. She practically told me to get on a plane.'

Then he got to the hard part. 'Gerry's parents and brother and sister were at the service and they told a few tales.'

'How did they seem.'

'Lost,' Steele said. 'Confused. I think the news of the twins is going to mean an awful lot to them.'

'Why did you go to the service, Steele?' she asked.

'Because I wanted to know more about the man whose children I want to raise and perhaps if they have questions I might be able to answer some,' he said. 'And I'm here because I love you,'

Candy looked at him and her eyes filled with tears. She realised then what Macey had meant when she'd asked her about duty.

Steele had no duty to her babies unless he wanted them.

They had been together for just two weeks when the news had hit.

He had every reason to walk away, to be gone, for things to fade out quietly, and yet he was here, sitting beside her and loving her with his eyes.

'I'm sorry they're—'

'You're going to say that once,' Steele broke in. 'Now. Then it's done.'

He was the most direct person she had ever met.

'You're sorry they're not mine?' he checked.

Tears shot out of her eyes without a sob. They just spilled out with such force that they splashed on her sarong.

'We have to be honest now,' he said. 'We have to

have the most honest conversation of our lives and I'm ringing in sick even if it take six months to sort this out because we're staying here till it's done.'

'We've only got five months left till they're here.'

'So we need to talk, right here, right now, and nothing, *nothing* gets left unsaid. My first thought, when you found out you were pregnant, was just that...I wanted them to be mine,' Steele said. 'Then I asked myself what would have happened if the twins weren't already here? My guess is that we'd have made it, because I was already coming to Hawaii and I don't go on holiday with women yet I was about to with you...'

She thought back. Things had been so easy then.

'And if we had made it, would you have wanted a baby at some stage?' he asked.

'I don't know. I think I would want children but if we couldn't...' She looked at Steele.

Did his infertility change how she felt about him?

Never.

Could she love him less?

Not a chance.

'If we couldn't have children we'd have gone for treatment,' Steele checked, and she nodded.

'Or adoption.'

'Okay,' he said. 'Had we adopted, would you have loved them less?'

'No!'

'Would you, in an argument, say that they weren't biologically mine?'

'No!'

'So what's the difference?'

'I don't know.'

'If we had to use donated sperm, would it change how we feel about them?'

'Of course not.'

'I'm going to be there for the pregnancy, the birth, the nappies. The twins will be mine,' Steele said. 'They will know about Gerry and when they turn into feral teenagers and say that I'm not their real father, I won't be hurt, not for a second. Instead, you and I will laugh in their moody, acne-laden faces when they say that, because we know we dealt with all that in Hawaii many, many years ago.'

Candy let out a breath.

'It's not just you that has concerns about getting married,' he said. 'I made a list of my own.' He took out his boarding pass and she read it.

Movies.
Football.
Cricket.

'It's a lot less complicated than mine,' she said.

'Oh, no, it isn't. I like my life very much and there are certain…er…requirements that I swore I would not forgo…'

She looked at him.

'The movies,' Steele explained. 'I like to go on my own sometimes. I just do. I don't want you saying, "But you used to take me"…'

Candy smiled.

'And I know it's horrible and selfish to take myself off when you'll have been stuck indoors with screaming twins, so perhaps you might like to take yourself off now and then to wherever ladies take themselves off to…'

'Like a spa day?' she said.

'I think so.'

'And you'd never say, "Oh, Candy, why do you have so many spa days? Why don't I come with you this time?"'

'Never,' he promised.

'Deal.'

'The football and cricket are one and the same…' He looked a bit worried and so too was Candy as she hated sport—it made her sweat and feel shaky and that was just watching it. 'I don't do romantic holidays,' he said. 'I shall, of course, and I'll do family ones too, but I have a group of friends and we like some big-ticket stuff.'

'Such as?'

'You remember how well we negotiated the movie issue?' Steele checked, because was he really going to land a perfect woman who didn't mind what he was about to suggest?

'I do.' Candy was very curious. She loved their discussions. 'What sort of big-ticket stuff?'

'International cricket events. World Cup…'

'Oh.'

'We don't always all go to everything.'

Candy said nothing at first. It really was a bit awkward. 'Would I be expected to go?'

'Well…' he said. 'There's a lot of drinking and singing…' He waited for her to say that no way would she ever want to go. Yes, this was awkward. 'Might be a bit of bad language, which wouldn't be great for the twins.' Still Candy said nothing and so he told her the real deal. 'There's also a very strict no-girlfriends-or-wives agreement, which I have, over the years, enforced on my friends several times. I'd never be able to live it down if I asked to bring you.'

He watched a little smile play on her lips.

'However,' he said quickly, 'I would think, given I'd be going away with friends for a couple of weeks now and then and leaving you, that you might need to escape with your girlfriends for a holiday every now and then, and I'd look after the twins and however many others we have...'

'Oh, I think I could agree to that.' Candy smiled and she looked at him, a man so happy in himself he wasn't looking for the other half. It had just turned out that she happened to be it. 'I love you, even without the twins, you do know that.'

'Why isn't there anything written about me on your list, then?' Steele asked, loving the way she blushed.

'I tried to write a letter.'

'Show me.'

'That's so unfair.'

'I need to know you love me, Candy,' he teased, and held out his hand.

It was so embarrassing as he sat there and read how crazy she was about him and then he started to laugh.

'"Friends with benefits." I'm sorry, Candy, this might be insensitive but if I'm having a friend with benefits then I want the blonde, leggy Candy. Not the heavily pregnant with twins one—that's husband stuff.' He looked at her. 'Marry me?'

'Honestly?'

'Honestly,' he said, his heart thumping in his chest. 'I want to be with you but I've never wanted to get married,' Candy admitted. 'I just don't want the big white wedding that my parents would insist on. I don't want to be standing there in a fluffy white dress pregnant with twins…'

'And you'd have to say your name out loud in a packed church,' he pointed out. 'And I'm a divorced heathen…' Then he smiled. 'We're in Hawaii, Candy. We can be married tomorrow, if that's what you want. I know it will upset your parents but I think they will be pleased as well.'

She started to smile.

'Is that a yes?' he checked. 'I'm starting to get worried here.'

'It's a very big yes,' she said. 'But won't your parents be disappointed to miss it?' Candy asked. After all, he was their only child.

'Yes,' he said, 'and I'll be tempted to point out that they missed most of my milestone events growing up, but I shan't do that, of course. They'll soon get over it, especially when they hear about the twins.'

They were back at the villa, all their lists checked and sorted. She loved their honesty, how they just spoke and worked it all out. 'We dealt with that very maturely.' Candy grinned in delight as she congratulated them.

'Oh, I can assure you that I don't feel very mature today,' Steele said. 'In fact, I want to do something very immature.'

He handed her the phone with a text from Annie, asking him if he'd had a think about her suggestion.

'This came through when I landed,' Steele explained. 'Can I?'

'Go on.' She smiled and watched as he started to type out a text.

There's nothing to think about or discuss. I am in Hawaii with Candy and we're about to get married. She's pregnant with twins, which means that she's very moody and volatile at the moment, so it's probably better that you don't text again. Regards, Steele.

He hit 'send' and with that he let go of the past and moved into the glorious future.

'You lied to me, though,' she said as they stepped into the villa and he took her in his arms.

'Never.'

'Yes, you did,' Candy said, and wrapped her hands around his neck. 'You said that the money you gave me had been lying around for five years, but it was only printed two years ago.'

Steele merely smiled at being caught. 'That's because I didn't want you worrying about taking food from your babies' mouths as you looked at that fantastic, sexy sarong.' He stroked her thick nipples through the fabric, and then he ran a tender hand over her stomach and his hand told her how sexy the changes were to him.

His kiss told her that too.

Her fabulous sarong dropped to the floor and Steele undressed with rapid ease.

The only thing missing from her perfect holiday had been her perfect man and now here he was, making love to her.

The doubts, the hesitation about whether or not he should intrude on her time here, were put to rest as he entered her. She wrapped herself around him, moved her body with his and held nothing back.

'I love you so much,' Candy said as she started to come.

No question, no hesitation, they both knew how precious the love they had was. Steele felt the roundness of her stomach press into his and he wanted to say he loved her back but she dragged him in so deep that all he could do was moan.

'I love you too,' he said afterwards as they lay there.

'You've still got red toenails.' She smiled as she looked at his feet next to hers.

'I was too embarrassed to buy nail-varnish remover,' he said. 'We'll need it if we're getting married on the beach.'

'Or not.'

'Oh, no.' Steele shook his head. 'We're getting it filmed for our families and a photo for Macey. I don't want everyone wondering if I'm secretly wearing your underwear.'

'Are we going to live in Kent?' Candy asked.

'We are,' Steele said. 'My offer's been accepted for that house. I wanted to ask you to marry me there,' he said. 'My plan was to do that when we looked through the house, except you chose not to come in.'

'You were going to ask me then?'

'Yes,' he said. 'But I didn't want to rush you.'

'So you gave me an extra five days?'

'I couldn't wait any longer,' Steele said, and then kissed the top of her head. 'So let's go and get the licence and get married so that the honeymoon can begin.'

It already had.

EPILOGUE

IT WAS, FOR CANDY, who had never wanted her own wedding, the perfect one.

It was, for Steele, who had sworn he would never marry again, the best wedding ever too.

Steele opted for sunset, though he didn't tell her why.

They walked to the beach together and stood, their bare feet caressed by the silky sand, Candy nervous, excited and all the things he made her feel as she faced him.

'Aloha,' he said, and she smiled. It was very hard to believe, after all their little teases about her holiday, that he was here with her and that this was their wedding.

'Aloha,' Candy said, grateful when he took her shaking hands.

The air smelt of coconut and frangipani. She was wearing a single flower in her hair. The breeze whipped her hair from her face and moulded Candy's dress to her soft curves. She had chosen a pale blue chiffon that was very simple and tied beneath her bust. He wore a linen suit, which was the colour of damp sand, and a white shirt and no nail varnish. He took her breath away and made her smile just as he had the moment they'd met.

She could hear the roar of the waves as they crashed onto the shore and then hissed back out to sea, leaving the sand as smooth, clean and pristine as their beckoning future.

As the huge crimson sun sank slowly into the sea the service started. They had decided on traditional vows—timeless and classic. She looked right at him as he placed the simple gold band they had chosen on her finger and Candy felt a soft shiver run through her as she heard the gorgeous, deep voice that had come into her life less than a month ago now vow to be with her for ever. 'With this ring I thee wed. With my body I thee worship.'

Then it was Candy's turn and her voice was very clear when she promised the same.

The sun had set, bamboo tiki torches lit the beach and the celebrant told them they were husband and wife.

'You may kiss your bride.'

Steele did and his kiss was long and lingering and then he moved his mouth to her ear. 'I'm the happiest I've ever been,' he said.

To hear those heartfelt words from Steele meant everything to Candy.

'I'm the happiest I've ever been too,' she agreed.

That was how they made each other feel.

With the service over and the documents signed, they walked hand in hand along the beach towards their villa with the waves lapping at their toes.

It was done, she was married and it was exactly as she'd wanted it to be, but as she saw the photographer taking down his equipment, even though they'd had the service filmed Candy felt a niggle of guilt that she had denied her parents this day.

Back in their suite she was determined to push the thought aside, but having again kissed his bride he pulled back and asked for her parents' number. 'You'll feel better when you've told them,' he said. 'You know you will.'

'They'll freak,' Candy said. 'I don't want to spoil today…' But she gave him the number and lay there with her eyes closed as a deep calm voice, one that was very used to dealing with upset, stubborn, set-in-their-ways people, introduced himself and told her father that he was a doctor who worked alongside Candy.

'No, there's nothing wrong with Candy or the babies,' Steele said, and then he told them how he had fallen in love with her, how he was going to take care of her, how he was completely fine about the twins and that they would be his. 'However,' Steele said, 'Gerry's parents will know…' He looked over at Candy. 'Candy and I have discussed it and we both agree that a baby can never have too many grandparents to love them.'

He spoke and listened and then said that he and Candy had got married today. Candy could hear her mother come onto the phone and the rise of drama that she'd dreaded ensued. She'd have to talk to them and deal with their recriminations and the guilt. She held her hand out for the phone but Steele simply listened to her mother and then spoke in that calm way of his and slowly the tension in her uncoiled.

'Candy didn't feel it appropriate, given that the pregnancy is already showing, to get married in a church, but we might renew our vows there.'

He dealt with the drama and examined his thumb-nail at one point as they droned on and on and then, finally, he smiled. 'Perhaps you'd like to tell your daughter that.' He handed her the phone. 'Your parents want to speak with you.'

She took the phone and braced herself for whatever her mother would fling at her and closed her eyes.

'Complimente...' her mother said, and it was so unexpected, so far from what she'd anticipated, that Candy burst into happy tears as her mother continued to speak. 'He sounds a nice man...'

'A very nice man,' Candy said.

A very nice man who was playing with her breasts and kissing her neck and was ready to get on with his honeymoon.

'Better?' Steele said as she hung up the phone.

'Is that why you wanted an evening wedding?'

'Yep. I didn't want to scare them calling late at night,' he said, 'and I knew you'd be worried.' He gave her a smile. 'Come here, Steele.'

'Steele?' Candy said, and then realised that was her surname now.

'Well, "Mrs Candida Steele", if you want to be formal.'

She was back to her dental commercial and smiling as he took her in his arms.

They were back to *before*.

* * * * *

MILLS & BOON®
Hardback – March 2015

ROMANCE

The Taming of Xander Sterne	Carole Mortimer
In the Brazilian's Debt	Susan Stephens
At the Count's Bidding	Caitlin Crews
The Sheikh's Sinful Seduction	Dani Collins
The Real Romero	Cathy Williams
His Defiant Desert Queen	Jane Porter
Prince Nadir's Secret Heir	Michelle Conder
Princess's Secret Baby	Carol Marinelli
The Renegade Billionaire	Rebecca Winters
The Playboy of Rome	Jennifer Faye
Reunited with Her Italian Ex	Lucy Gordon
Her Knight in the Outback	Nikki Logan
Baby Twins to Bind Them	Carol Marinelli
The Firefighter to Heal Her Heart	Annie O'Neil
Thirty Days to Win His Wife	Andrea Laurence
Her Forbidden Cowboy	Charlene Sands
The Blackstone Heir	Dani Wade
After Hours with Her Ex	Maureen Child

MEDICAL

Tortured by Her Touch	Dianne Drake
It Happened in Vegas	Amy Ruttan
The Family She Needs	Sue MacKay
A Father for Poppy	Abigail Gordon

MILLS & BOON®
Large Print – March 2015

ROMANCE

A Virgin for His Prize	Lucy Monroe
The Valquez Seduction	Melanie Milburne
Protecting the Desert Princess	Carol Marinelli
One Night with Morelli	Kim Lawrence
To Defy a Sheikh	Maisey Yates
The Russian's Acquisition	Dani Collins
The True King of Dahaar	Tara Pammi
The Twelve Dates of Christmas	Susan Meier
At the Chateau for Christmas	Rebecca Winters
A Very Special Holiday Gift	Barbara Hannay
A New Year Marriage Proposal	Kate Hardy

HISTORICAL

Darian Hunter: Duke of Desire	Carole Mortimer
Rescued by the Viscount	Anne Herries
The Rake's Bargain	Lucy Ashford
Unlaced by Candlelight	Various
The Warrior's Winter Bride	Denise Lynn

MEDICAL

A Secret Shared...	Marion Lennox
Flirting with the Doc of Her Dreams	Janice Lynn
The Doctor Who Made Her Love Again	Susan Carlisle
The Maverick Who Ruled Her Heart	Susan Carlisle
After One Forbidden Night...	Amber McKenzie
Dr Perfect on Her Doorstep	Lucy Clark

MILLS & BOON®
Hardback – April 2015

ROMANCE

The Billionaire's Bridal Bargain	Lynne Graham
At the Brazilian's Command	Susan Stephens
Carrying the Greek's Heir	Sharon Kendrick
The Sheikh's Princess Bride	Annie West
His Diamond of Convenience	Maisey Yates
Olivero's Outrageous Proposal	Kate Walker
The Italian's Deal for I Do	Jennifer Hayward
Virgin's Sweet Rebellion	Kate Hewitt
The Millionaire and the Maid	Michelle Douglas
Expecting the Earl's Baby	Jessica Gilmore
Best Man for the Bridesmaid	Jennifer Faye
It Started at a Wedding...	Kate Hardy
Just One Night?	Carol Marinelli
Meant-To-Be Family	Marion Lennox
The Soldier She Could Never Forget	Tina Beckett
The Doctor's Redemption	Susan Carlisle
Wanted: Parents for a Baby!	Laura Iding
His Perfect Bride?	Louisa Heaton
Twins on the Way	Janice Maynard
The Nanny Plan	Sarah M. Anderson

MILLS & BOON®
Large Print – April 2015

ROMANCE

Taken Over by the Billionaire	Miranda Lee
Christmas in Da Conti's Bed	Sharon Kendrick
His for Revenge	Caitlin Crews
A Rule Worth Breaking	Maggie Cox
What The Greek Wants Most	Maya Blake
The Magnate's Manifesto	Jennifer Hayward
To Claim His Heir by Christmas	Victoria Parker
Snowbound Surprise for the Billionaire	Michelle Douglas
Christmas Where They Belong	Marion Lennox
Meet Me Under the Mistletoe	Cara Colter
A Diamond in Her Stocking	Kandy Shepherd

HISTORICAL

Strangers at the Altar	Marguerite Kaye
Captured Countess	Ann Lethbridge
The Marquis's Awakening	Elizabeth Beacon
Innocent's Champion	Meriel Fuller
A Captain and a Rogue	Liz Tyner

MEDICAL

It Started with No Strings...	Kate Hardy
One More Night with Her Desert Prince...	Jennifer Taylor
Flirting with Dr Off-Limits	Robin Gianna
From Fling to Forever	Avril Tremayne
Dare She Date Again?	Amy Ruttan
The Surgeon's Christmas Wish	Annie O'Neil

MILLS & BOON®

Why shop at millsandboon.co.uk?

Each year, thousands of romance readers find their perfect read at millsandboon.co.uk. That's because we're passionate about bringing you the very best romantic fiction. Here are some of the advantages of shopping at www.millsandboon.co.uk:

* **Get new books first**—you'll be able to buy your favourite books one month before they hit the shops

* **Get exclusive discounts**—you'll also be able to buy our specially created monthly collections, with up to 50% off the RRP

* **Find your favourite authors**—latest news, interviews and new releases for all your favourite authors and series on our website, plus ideas for what to try next

* **Join in**—once you've bought your favourite books, don't forget to register with us to rate, review and join in the discussions

Visit **www.millsandboon.co.uk** for all this and more today!